DUNGEON DRAGON

EMMA LAYBOURN

ANDERSEN PRESS • LONDON

To the children of Moss Hey School

First published in 2008 by
Andersen Press Limited,
20 Vauxhall Bridge Road, London SW1V 2SA

British Library Cataloguing in Publication Data available

ISBN 978 184 270 736 4

Mixed Sources
Product group from well-managed
forests and other controlled sources
www.fsc.org Cert no. TT-COC-0002227
© 1996 Forest Stewardship Council

Typeset by FiSH Books, Enfield, Middx.
Printed and bound in Great Britain by
CPI Bookmarque, Croydon, CR0 4TD

1

Rab

They were on their way to market, a dangerous place.

Rab was glad of it. He couldn't wait to get there.

He'd had enough of the farm. He'd been stuck for too long amongst boring sheep and turnips. Danger enticed him like a huge bowl of ice cream, sweet and shocking enough to make him gasp – to make everybody gasp. He was ready to amaze the world with his daring.

Now his chance had come. Rab grinned in anticipation. Until last month, a trip to market had been as dull as digging turnips; but things had changed. Fear filled the town. Rumours of magical demons crept through the streets. The market was especially perilous, because it could be so easily spied on from the lofty towers of the Glass Palace: the palace of the Sorcerer.

His sister Freya dragged her feet. 'Surely we can wait till next week,' she pleaded.

'We can't wait! We need to sell the cow before it's too

lame to walk,' insisted Rab. 'And what about Gran's shoes? They're all in pieces. Gran has to have new shoes.'

'I suppose,' sighed Freya. She glanced back despondently at their little farmhouse perched on its crooked hillside. Down below it, almost hidden in the valley, the deep, silver river was a gleaming ribbon trying to pull her home.

Rab didn't look back. The promise of adventure tugged him forward. The farm and the river had trapped their father and killed him; he wasn't going to end up like *that*. He aimed to be a hero like his grandpa, to live and die by the sword.

His hand fumbled for the hilt of his grandfather's long knife, stuck in his belt. Although it was rather short for a hero's sword, at the feel of it his heart quickened. Great deeds waited to be done.

'Oh, come on!' he said impatiently, stopping yet again to let the others catch up. It wasn't just Freya who was slow; the cow was too lame to go any faster, Holman the farmhand was too frightened, and Saintly Gran's donkey was too depressed.

'I shouldn't have come,' said Holman heavily. His pudgy face was sweating. 'Not feeling well.' He coughed, pointedly.

'You can have a nice sit down at the market,' Freya reassured him. 'It might be back to normal now. The Sorcerer must stop sometime, after all.' She tried to smile. 'If he posts up any more Rules, he'll run out of walls to stick them on!'

'He won't stop,' Rab declared with certainty.

'Why not? The Rules started up out of the blue. The Sorcerer might drop them any time. He might have only done it for a joke,' suggested Freya.

'Some joke,' muttered Holman. 'No pies?'

'Exactly. He must be joking. Why else make a Rule like that?'

'Because he's mad,' said Rab, with satisfaction.

Holman's pasty face clouded in alarm. 'Careful – he'll hear you!'

'Good!'

'But remember what happened to your poor grandpa!' warned Holman, with a glance at Saintly Gran, dozing on the donkey.

'Oh, I do,' said Rab, his hand tightening on the hilt of his knife.

'But you don't want to end up like him!'

'I don't intend to. Now can we get a move on, *please*?'

As they neared the town, their dusty path met other dusty paths. Like the spokes of a spider's web, all were drawn inexorably towards the centre – towards the marketplace overlooked by the high, glittering glass towers.

There he sits, thought Rab, crouched like a spider awaiting its prey. Rab had no idea what the Sorcerer looked like. All he knew was that he lurked amongst the shining spires of the Glass Palace.

Gran woke up. 'Cobblestones!' she cried. 'We're there! I can smell the market.' Nearly blind and almost deaf, she prided herself on her other senses' sharpness. She wrinkled her nose at the smell, but did not complain. Gran never complained; she was famous for it.

The market was two-thirds empty. Freya chose one of many unclaimed stalls, and set out their wares: the cracked eggs (Gran had dropped the basket), the sweating cheeses, the hanks of greasy wool. The cow sighed, and waited on three legs.

'Things haven't got better at all,' said Rab delightedly. 'I told you so!'

The clothes stall had turned grey. No patch of brightness peeped from its layers of lead-hued shirts. The baker had plenty of plain bread, but no cakes, no tarts, no pies or buns. The fruit stall held mostly cabbage.

Many stalls had disappeared completely. There were no sweets for sale; no charms, no trinkets, no mirrors, no books, no toys. People stood in uneasy clumps, glancing at the sky. The rainbowed shadow of the palace fell across the cobbles, netting them in multi-coloured light.

Rab looked at the walls. They were white with paper, yards and yards of it pasted on every surface.

'They can't all be Rules!' gasped Freya, horrified.

'They can,' said Rab. 'What did I tell you? Mad!' Walking briskly over to the wall, he began to read aloud.

NEW RULES OF THE CITY,
by Royal Decree

18th INSTALMENT

Number 239 *No jokes.*
Number 240 *No feather beds.*
Number 241 *No whistling.*
*This includes tin whistles, which are already
BANNED in any case. (see Rule 67(d))*
Number 242 *No pets, except guide dogs for the
blind.*
Number 243 *Nothing to be worn in the hair
except string (brown).*
Number 244 *No bacon.*
Number 245 *No guide dogs for the blind.*
What's wrong with a white stick anyway?
Number 246 *Beans and cabbage every Tuesday.*

By Order of His Bountiful Majesty
TARCORAX,
High Sorcerer, Lord of the Glass Palace, Master of the Dominions.
REMEMBER! THE AIR HAS EYES AND EARS.

'Does it now!' said Rab. His gaze moved upwards from the wall, past the huddled rooftops to the great glass towers that leaned against the racing clouds. All his life, he had looked on the Glass Palace with jealous fascination. If he stared at it for long enough, the world would seem to tip suddenly upside down and the spires become a cluster of gigantic icicles, hanging over a well of sky.

The glass depths of the palace were green, as cloudy as an iceberg – but not frozen; deep inside its ramparts, formless shadows stirred. Above its vast buttresses, tower climbed on crystal tower to the highest pinnacle of all: the Tower of Tarcorax.

A sudden light flashed from the topmost turret, half-blinding Rab. Perhaps the Sorcerer himself was there! Hidden behind his walls of glass, spying on the marketplace – on *him*. Rab squared his shoulders.

'Stupid Rules!' he said loudly.

'What's that?' enquired Gran. 'What's the matter, Rab?'

'More Rules, Gran. Why should *he* tell us what to do?'

'The old Rules made some sense,' said Holman. 'No fishing out of other people's ponds, no short-changing, no singing after midnight—'

'Nobody obeyed the old Rules,' pointed out Freya, hurriedly untying the ribbon from her hair and wondering where to find some string (brown).

'Didn't matter,' said Holman. 'They didn't get picked up for it. Not like now.' He shuddered.

'And now?' demanded Rab. He was gaining an audience, as people turned to listen. 'What's the point of the Rules now? No singing at all, let alone after midnight! No dancing, no football, no flags, no swimming no games no gardens no parties—'

'No poetry,' murmured Freya wistfully, as he paused for breath.

'–no stories no cakes no puddings no jokes no puzzles no plays—'

'No whistling,' said Holman mournfully. 'That's bad. I mean – whistling is bad – bad thing to do. Wicked. Obviously.' He glanced around anxiously.

'The Sorcerer's gone crazy!' Rab announced.

'All right,' whispered Freya, 'just don't shout about it.' She tried to take his arm, but Rab shook her away.

'Crazy!' he cried, more loudly. The stallholders nudged each other. 'He's out of his mind!'

'Hold your tongue, Rab lad!' said a rope-seller sharply. 'Don't you know what happens to people who talk that way?'

Rab threw back his head defiantly. 'I know, all right! My grandpa died in the dungeons of the Sorcerer – just because he dared ask him a favour. One little favour! And he got thrown into chains for it. But I'm not scared of Tarcorax! I'm not afraid of speaking out! It's time *someone* did!'

Every startled eye was on him now. The roper tapped a warning finger on his lips, but Rab ignored him. Holman whimpered faintly. Only Saintly Gran on her donkey was patiently unheeding.

Rab stormed on. 'What does Tarcorax think he's doing? He hasn't bothered with the Rules for years – then all of a sudden the walls are plastered with this nonsense! He's gone mad! No birthdays? No gardens? Where's the sense in that?'

'Something's gone wrong,' said Freya.

'Something *will* go wrong,' the roper muttered grimly, 'if you don't shut your brother up.'

Freya gazed up at the rooftops. She thought she saw a shimmer in the air. 'Rab!' she said urgently. 'Hush, now! We've got a cow to sell, and what about Gran's shoes?'

'Who cares about a cow? Who cares about new shoes?' cried her brother. 'Are we men or mice? Why does nobody stand up and challenge Tarcorax?'

'Oh Rab, oh no, not here, not now,' wailed Freya.

'Nowt to do with *me*,' said Holman. 'I'm out of here.' He backed away, along with everyone else, leaving an empty space around Rab. The roper began to pile up his coils of rope, squinting nervously at the sky.

The shimmer above the roofs was growing stronger. The air quivered as if in the heat. Ripples of faint colour began to run through it.

'Quiet now, there's a good lad! Simmer down!' said the roper in a frantic undertone. 'Do you *want* to end up in front of the Sorcerer?'

'There's nothing I'd like better! Then I could tell him just what I think of his idiotic laws—'

'Oh don't, Rab, don't!' breathed Freya.

'–and let him know what an arrogant, crazy, stupid tyrant he really is!'

8

High above Rab the air fizzed and exploded, twice. Two shapes dropped swiftly out of the sky. Freya had a brief glimpse of leathery wings, wide, smirking grins and long flickering tails, before the air wrapped itself back round them with a hollow gulping sound. They were gone as if they'd never been there.

And so was Rab.

2

Freya

'Was that lightning, dear?' asked Gran. 'Is it a storm?'

'You can't say we didn't warn him,' sighed the roper wearily. 'Those demons listen everywhere.'

Freya stared first at the scorch marks on the cobblestones, then up at the sky. There was a faint smell of sulphur. Not a trace of a shimmer.

'Where is he?' she whispered. 'Where have they taken him?'

Without looking up, the roper nodded at the Glass Palace. 'Under there. If he's lucky.'

'*Under?*'

'Down in the dungeons.'

'And what if he's unlucky?'

'Then they'll take him to see the Sorcerer first.'

'Oh, Rab! I have to go after him!'

'You can't do that! Steady on now.' He patted her awkwardly on the shoulder. 'Try not to fret. Maybe the Sorcerer will go light on him, seeing as he's only a lad. A brave lad.'

'He's kept talking about the Sorcerer for weeks,' said Freya, 'going on about fighting for justice. I never thought he'd do *this*.'

'Well, now. He's a plucky lad. A hero, if you like.'

'Our grandpa was a hero,' said Freya unhappily. 'And *he* died trying to dig his way out of the Sorcerer's dungeons, when his tunnel collapsed on top of him. Gran's told us all about him, loads of times.' Freya knew the hateful tale by heart.

'Trying to dig his way out?' said the roper, staring. 'But how does she... Ah well, never mind. She's a brave lady, your gran. She's had a lot to put up with in her life. I never heard that tale about your grandpa, but your gran's told us many a time about the sacrifices she's had to make.'

'Oh, yes,' murmured Freya, who had heard about them many a time too.

'Bringing up the pair of you, and running your farm, ever since your father died. Everyone knows what a saint your gran is. And how she's suffered with her eyes... Yet even now she can't see or hear, she's still doing all the cooking and the washing for you, isn't she? With no help from anyone. What a brave lady.'

'Holman helps,' said Freya. But when she turned to look for him, Holman had disappeared, leaving the cow's halter in Gran's wrinkled hand.

'It's very quiet today,' remarked Gran, peering around weakly. 'Business isn't what is used to be. I blame that Sorcerer.'

'Hush, Gran!' whispered Freya.

'What, dear?'

'*Sssh!*' said Freya loudly.

'I see,' said Gran. 'Nobody wants to listen to a poor old lady. But I don't complain. I suppose a chair is too much to ask. And could Rab get me a cup of tea?'

'Rab's gone... to see a friend, Gran,' yelled Freya.

'A friend? But who'll sell the cow?'

'I will.'

'You?' Gran wrinkled her nose doubtfully.

'Not today you won't.' The roper shook his head. 'Nobody'll buy it off you now, in case it brings – well, bad luck. Nobody wants trouble, you see.'

'Isn't there a way into the palace?' begged Freya. 'Isn't there any way I can get to Rab?'

He shook his head. 'The only way in is to be captured by the demons. You don't want that. Anyway, if they take you, what happens to your gran? She's your responsibility now. You've got to look after her.'

'Gran needs new shoes,' said Freya numbly. 'I can't buy shoes unless I sell the cow.'

'I'll give you a bit of rope to stick on the soles,' he said kindly. 'They'll do for indoors, and I don't suppose she does much outside these days, does she?'

'No. We do it all.' The milking, the shearing, the digging, the fencing, the chopping, the walling, the sowing, the reaping. Now there was no Rab to help, and from the look of it, no Holman either.

'She's a saint, your gran,' said the rope-seller. 'You never hear her complain. Get her home safely, now! That brother of yours will turn up soon enough, I

12

daresay: the Sorcerer won't be able to lock up a brave young lad like him for long.'

'My gran's a saint, my brother's a hero,' recited Freya, as if it were a lesson she must remember.

'That's right! You should be proud of them both.'

3

Tower

Rab's eyes were full of yellow smoke. His nose was full of the stink of sulphur. A deafening wind roared right through his head from one ear to the other. Beneath his feet, he could feel nothing at all; but around his upper arms were clamped cold, hard hands like shackles of stone.

Without warning, they released him. He tumbled onto an unyielding floor. As the smoke cleared, Rab saw two demons twirling their tails at him, and grinning.

He coughed and sat up, rubbing his eyes. 'Where am I?'

'Oh, you're here all right!' they squealed in high, whiny voices. 'Tower of Tarcorax. Where you wanted.'

'But it's *dark*,' said Rab in bewilderment. How could this be the Glass Palace? Where was the blaze of sunlight pouring through the crystal walls, the fabled view for forty miles in each direction?

There were no views at all.

The walls were so thickly wrapped in layers of

14

tapestries, so shrouded in curtains and hangings, that Rab couldn't detect even a glimmer of daylight. A huge chandelier dotted with crooked candles hung from the glass ceiling, but only a few of the candles were lit. The ceiling was black with soot.

And he was surrounded by statues made of glass.

Rab stood up unsteadily. The room swam before his eyes. As he moved, everything seemed to shift, as if he were inside a jigsaw – a glass jigsaw of a jungle. Glass antelopes, glass tigers, glass bears and lions and unicorns and gryphons; wherever the candlelight touched them, it splintered into a thousand rainbow pieces. It gave him a headache.

A single piece of plainness caught his eye. He rested his gaze there, for relief. It was a large, brown rectangle that leaned against one wall, a piece of string tied across it from one side to the other. He realised it was the back of a picture, its face turned away.

'Here you are, Master! You'll like this one!' announced one of the demons chirpily. 'He thinks you're an arrogant crazy tyrant.'

'Arrogant crazy *stupid* tyrant,' corrected the other demon, with a leer. 'Haven't bothered all these years, and now you've gone mad. Hee, hee.'

'We're off to find some more. *Lots* of whistlers about.'

The two of them fizzed away and were gone.

'Haven't *bothered*?' roared a voice behind Rab.

He spun round. From behind a glass gryphon, the Sorcerer strode forward.

'Haven't bothered! Well, that's just typical. The years

I've spent slaving away for these thankless people! Sleepless nights worrying about taxes, endless days listening to petitions when I could have been doing my magic. Wearing myself to a shravel! Well, I've had enough of it. D'you hear?'

Rab gaped at Tarcorax's cloak. A silver blaze of minuscule moons and stars, it looked as if it had been woven by demented silkworms. Tarcorax himself was short, for a wizard. His beard was all wrong too: not white and flowing, but red and bristly as a fox, as were his hair and eyebrows. He had no sword, and his staff was only made of glass. Rab's spirits rose.

The Sorcerer was staring at Rab's feet.

'Shoelaces,' he muttered. 'I haven't banned shoelaces yet. That's next.'

'People's shoes will fall off!'

'Good point,' growled Tarcorax. 'Losing shoes will become a criminal offence.'

'But that's ridiculous! All your Rules are ridiculous!'

Tarcorax poked irritably with his staff at the carpet, until its pattern began to writhe and flow.

'Ridiculous?' he rasped. 'Yes, of course they are. They are made for ridiculous people.'

'But they're stupid!'

'*Precisely*,' said Tarcorax. He glared at the picture propped against the wall and growled under his breath. A wisp of purple smoke began to waft around it.

'No one laughs at *me*,' muttered the Sorcerer.

'But somebody's got to tell you—'

'Be quiet!' Still glowering at the wall, Tarcorax raised

his staff. There was a faint, deep hum as if a thousand bees had awoken in the depths of the palace. The purple smoke darkened, and curled a little tighter around the picture. It curled and swayed as if wondering which way to go.

'Listen to me!' yelled Rab. 'You wouldn't listen to my grandfather, but you're going to listen to me!'

'Your grandfather?' said Tarcorax without interest.

'He came to seek your help, twelve years ago!'

'Did I help him?'

'You had him thrown into the dungeons,' said Rab bitterly.

'Really? I don't remember...but then, I've had so many people thrown into the dungeons. After all, what else are dungeons for?' Tarcorax stared intently at the twisting smoke, which began to twine like a snake, curling itself into shapes, letters, almost spelling out a word...

Rab marched round, planted himself in front of the Sorcerer, hands on hips, and said very loudly, 'You can't imprison innocent people, just because they don't follow your stupid Rules!'

The purple smoke reared up and dissolved away. Tarcorax banged down his staff in exasperation. 'What else are Rules for?' he roared. 'Tell me this. Are the people starving?'

'No, not exactly, but—'

'Not at all! They're getting a good plain diet. Cakes and sweets are bad for them. Are they sick? Are they hurt?'

'Well, no—'

'So what are you complaining about?'

'We can't live like this!' cried Rab. 'You're taking away everything that makes life pleasant and easy – everything that makes life worth living! The Rules are just crazy! You've gone mad, and I'm here to stop you. *En garde!*' With a flourish he had practised many times before the mirror, he pulled out his grandfather's knife and pointed it at the Sorcerer's chest. It gleamed as bright as dawn.

At the side of the Sorcerer, the glass gryphon raised itself slowly to its feet. It had the body of a lion, the wings of a horse, the face of an eagle.

'Don't call him mad,' it whispered. 'He is a genius.'

'All right, all right!' snapped Tarcorax. 'I don't need *you* to defend me!' He turned back to Rab, eyes glittering. 'Put that thing away, for heaven's sake. What on earth is it – a carving knife?'

'This is my sword,' said Rab proudly. He slashed the knife through the air and jabbed it at the Sorcerer's shoulder. 'And with it I will wreak vengeance on you!'

'No, you won't,' said Tarcorax, and twitched his staff. The knife changed colour, then had no colour at all. Rab could see right through it. The blade had turned to glass, as clear as water until a cloud of fine cracks ran over it from tip to hilt. With a rustle like crumpled paper, it shattered into tiny, glittering fragments on the floor. Rab stared down at them in dismay.

'You will obey the Rules,' snarled Tarcorax, 'or be cast into the dungeons. They are *my* Rules, and I am the

Ruler. By the stars, I'll make you obey me! I *will* be obeyed!' He thumped his staff on the ground until it sang like a tuning fork. 'I will *not* be laughed at! That was my very first Rule – no laughing. Pleasant and easy? Why should you have pleasure and ease? Why should you laugh? Why should *you* be happy?' he cried. He wasn't looking at Rab.

He kicked his staff across the room.

'Where are you?' he bellowed.

With a flash and a pop, the two demons reappeared, smirking, at his shoulder.

'Here, Master!'

'Not *you* – oh, it doesn't matter. Take him away.' Tarcorax gestured impatiently at Rab.

'Dungeons?'

'Where else?'

'Only they're getting a teensy bit full...'

'So?'

'There's only the potato cellar still empty...'

'So?' Tarcorax's beard bristled, and the grins wilted on the demons' faces.

'Hang on!' Rab protested. 'I haven't finished yet!'

'Oh yes, you have,' snarled Tarcorax. '*Dungeons.*'

And all at once Rab's eyes were full of smoke, and his nose was full of sulphur.

4

Dungeon

The first thing about the dungeon was that it had no door. The demons dumped him and fizzed off without any need of an entrance. Rab sneezed away the sulphur, and looked around.

It was fully as cold and grim as he had ever dreamed. It smelled of damp earth. Although the walls were made of glass, they were so stained with mould and dirt that they might as well have been stone. The glass ceiling was scarcely any cleaner: through it struggled the only light, a murky green glow. It was like being at the bottom of a pond.

There was nobody else there. No long-forgotten, mouldering prisoner to croak a greeting: no skeleton manacled to the wall. No ghost of a grandfather.

'But I *am* a hero's grandson!' said Rab aloud. 'I'm *not* just a farmer's boy!'

He'd heard Gran's wonderful tale about his brave grandpa so many times over the years. He knew it by heart: how, when Gran started to go blind, Grandpa sold everything he had, right down to his shoes, and walked barefoot to the Palace with a bag of gold. How he asked the Sorcerer to take the gold in exchange for a cure for Gran, and was refused. How he challenged the Sorcerer to fight a duel for the spell he needed.

And how he so nearly won, until Tarcorax tried to flee and cheated by breaking his glass door into pieces. Grandpa was lamed by stepping on the broken glass, captured, and thrown into the dungeon...

Each time he'd heard it, Rab had thought, I'll be a hero like him one day. Better! I would make the Sorcerer listen! I'd wear some shoes! I wouldn't let my escape tunnel collapse over my head! Not me.

And now here he was.

Rab studied the floor, which Grandpa was supposed to have dug through. Instead of glass, it was made of large, smooth flagstones, with pale toadstools sprouting through the cracks. This really was the very bottom of the palace; tons of glass above, and nothing beneath but earth.

On the flagstones lay a clammy blanket and a jug of water. In one corner, behind a ragged curtain, was a black hole in the floor, a rather terrifying toilet. In the opposite corner lay a small pile of potatoes. Surely, thought Rab, those weren't his rations?

No – for there was a hatch in the wall, too narrow for escape but large enough to let through a lump of bread, which stood on the ledge below it. Rab peered through the hatch, but all was dark.

And there was no door.

'Well,' said Rab. 'At least I told him. Somebody had to tell him.' The words echoed dully around the empty dungeon.

He sat on the shabby blanket and replayed the scene with Tarcorax in his head. It was too short; Tarcorax had given him no time. It needed editing. In Rab's new, revised version, Tarcorax staggered back, crying,

'No one has ever dared defy me thus! What is your name, boy?' and regarded him with wild-eyed wonder.

'Never mind my name,' declared Rab, 'but beware my blade!'

The Sorcerer's eyes narrowed. His contemptuous laugh was tinged with fear. 'You dare fight *me*? On your own head be it!'

This time Rab's sword was long and sharp, and did not get turned to glass. Tarcorax flung back his cloak and unsheathed his own weapon. The demons gibbered, terrified, in a corner, as steel clashed on steel.

The fight in Rab's head went on for a long time. He worked out all his moves in detail. His shirt was in tatters and streaked with blood before the fight was over; but at last the Sorcerer was pinned against the wall and begging for mercy. Rab wasn't quite sure what happened after that.

Well, it could have gone that way, decided Rab. Maybe he'd given the Sorcerer food for thought, at least. Perhaps Tarcorax would brood on his words and call for him again. The next time they met, things would be different.

He waited. No call came. The silence began to ring in

22

his ears. After a while Rab jumped up, seized the bread and forced himself to eat it. Although it was stale, it was better than silence.

Then he paced around his dungeon, measuring it out, because that was what prisoners did. It only took him six strides from one corner to the next.

At the third corner Rab stopped, frowned, and picked up a potato.

Potato?

The truth hit him with the indignant splat of a mud pie in the face. This wasn't even a proper dungeon. He was a prisoner in the potato cellar.

5

Cellar

That was the longest night of Rab's life.

He spent much of it raging at the Sorcerer. *Potato cellar?* Didn't Tarcorax know who he was dealing with? Didn't he recognise a hero when he saw one? You didn't lock a hero in the potato cellar! Devising horrible humiliations for the Sorcerer, he finally fell asleep.

He awoke to a clunk and a strong smell of mutton and turnip. A bowl of soup had appeared in the hatch. After Rab had gulped it down, he felt a little better. He'd soon find a way out of here. Then he'd teach Tarcorax to dump him in a potato cellar...

He walked around it once again, checking carefully for cracks in the filthy walls. There were plenty, but none was any thicker than a hair.

The flagstones looked more promising, for the cracks between them were wider. Rab knelt and prised at them with his fingers, skinning all his knuckles, but without result. The smallest stone probably weighed more than he did, and he had nothing to use as a lever.

How on earth had Grandpa dug his way through these? If one of the flagstones had toppled over onto Grandpa, it was no wonder he'd died trying to tunnel out...

Rab sighed. If he were trapped in a proper dungeon, he would find a way out, no problem. But how could a hero be expected to escape from a potato cellar?

He slumped down on his blanket again to wait. Although he was no longer sure what he was waiting for, waiting was the only thing left to do. The cellar offered no other occupation, apart from juggling potatoes.

He should be planting his own potatoes this week, back on the farm. Freya was bound to forget. Rab wondered how much she'd got for the cow; probably not enough. And who was looking after Gran now he wasn't there?

Worries began to froth up in his head like bubbles in a shaken bottle, until he felt his skull would burst with them.

First, he worried that Gran would fall down the well. He'd been promising to mend its broken cover for months, but had never got round to it... Now the thought of the well knocked at his conscience like the wind banging a gate. On the second night, it woke him every half hour with a guilty start.

On the third day, Rab managed to forget about the well. Instead, he worried that Holman wouldn't bother to milk the cows. Their reproachful moos echoed through his imagination.

On the fourth day, he worried that his dutiful sister Freya would forget to feed the hens. She'd fed them daily for the last three years, but might well go to pieces without Rab there.

On the fifth day, he worried that Gran would try to chop the wood and slice her foot off with the axe. Blood spurted through his broken dreams.

On the sixth day, he stormed up and down a good deal, yelling curses at the Sorcerer and punching the air many times with his fists. He punched a wall, as well, but only once.

On the seventh day, he huddled, shivering, in a corner with his blanket, using the potatoes as a lumpy pillow, trying to think about nothing at all.

He really, really wanted a warm bath. He was sick of bread and water. The mutton soup had stopped two days ago; boring though it had been, he now longed to have it back. And he wished there *was* a skeleton manacled to the wall. A skeleton would have been company. Rab had never felt so abandoned and alone, not even when his father died.

Maybe he was destined to die here, lonely and forgotten, to turn into a skeleton himself when the bread ran out . . . This was the end of all his hopes. He was buried as deep as Grandpa.

Sleep would not come. Rab's limbs were aching and he shuddered uncontrollably with cold. He was still awake when the gloomy pond light filtering through the ceiling warned him of another hopeless dawn.

Rab groaned, dragging his blanket tighter round his shoulders, and forced his weary eyes to open.

Then he stiffened, staring at the footprints on the floor.

Footprints? No, impossible! They must be dirty markings on the flagstones, streaks of grime. They weren't really walking across the cell towards him, not at all...

Or they were his own footprints, that was it. It was the gloomy, grey dawn light that made them look so big, much bigger than they should be. The way they appeared out of the wall was simply an illusion. There was nothing strange about them. They were just his footprints. Nothing to do with the old tales.

Rab's heart seemed to stop. Nothing to do with the Dawn Walker. Nothing at all. The Dawn Walker didn't exist...

As he gazed down, unable to stop shivering, the light dwindled. The cell grew foggy, thick with twilight closing round him. He could hardly feel. So cold. He could hardly see...

His eyes began to close.

Suddenly the dungeon was lit up by a blinding flash. Rab was knocked backwards: the grey fog was blown away. There was a stink of sulphur, a demon's giggle and a thud. Rab was no longer alone.

6

Farm

After the rain, the hillsides around Withy Farm blazed like a tumbled tablecloth, jewelled and embroidered. The grass gleamed emerald in the sun. The wheat was as yellow as topaz, sewn with ruby poppies and sapphire cornflowers.

Down in its valley, the river sparkled like a string of diamonds, while a mother-of-pearl rainbow buried itself in the middle of the Long Meadow. Eight miles over to the west, the Glass Palace glittered like a miniature treasure-heap piled on the horizon.

This was nothing to Freya. All she saw was the milking shed looming up twice a day, the gaps in the tumbledown walls leering at her, the loose thatch on the roof waving madly for attention, and the ranks of overgrown vegetables dying to be picked. No sooner had she harvested one row of beans than the next withered and fell over.

Every now and then she looked for Rab, who should be wandering back home along the winding lane, as he usually did after a day's fishing, flicking off grass-heads with a stick. He was never there.

At least the lidless eye of the well no longer stared at her accusingly. Although Rab had kept telling her to leave the job for him, fixing the well-cover had been the second thing she'd done, straight after she soled Gran's shoes.

'Where's Rab?' asked Gran, for the fourth time that day.

Freya shrugged. She'd run out of excuses. At first Rab had been away fishing, then buying a horse, then visiting friends. Now he was just out. She couldn't face shouting the complicated truth into Gran's ear. How could you tell a saint bad news?

'I hope he's not done anything rash, like his dear grandpa. Do you know, when your grandpa set off to see the Sorcerer, he didn't tell a soul where he was going. Over hill, over dale, he tramped, in his bare feet, with his bag of gold clanking in his pocket ...'

Saintly Gran settled herself more comfortably in her chair.

'All to end up in the dungeons,' she said. 'All his journey, all his labour, just to end up in the dungeons. Left to starve,' she said. 'Left to tunnel out in desperation with his bare, bleeding fingers. To have the breath squeezed out of him by tons of earth and crushing stone—'

Freya made a dive for the door. Too fast; Gran caught her movement.

'Where's Holman?' she asked querulously.

'Gone,' yelled Freya.

'Gone where?'

'To find another job,' Freya shouted. She'd had a letter. Holman had gone to work for a farm six miles upriver, well away from sorcerers and demons.

Gran could not hear her. 'What? It's not his day off,' she grumbled. 'Who'll fetch the wood? I don't complain, Freya, but the fire's getting low.'

'I'll do it,' said Freya. She shouldered the axe.

'Freya? There's no milk for supper.'

'When I've chopped the wood, Gran.'

'Freya? There's no water left in the jug.'

'I'll fetch some in a minute, Gran.'

'Freya? How long will you be? I don't complain, but I'm getting very thirsty.'

'Not long, Gran.'

Freya went outside to the well. She lifted the mended cover and stared into its black depths.

She could just walk out. Disappear, as Rab had done; as her grandfather had done. She could shed her old life like an awkward, heavy coat, leave it all behind. She could do it now. Put down the bucket, and go. No need to stay trapped in her dungeon of duty.

The inside of the well was cold as death. Freya hauled up a gallon of icy water, lugged the heavy, dripping pail back to the house and filled the jug for Gran.

Then she swung the axe with blistered hands. *Thunk*, went the wood.

'Milk the cows,' she muttered. 'Clean out the cow shed.' *Thunk*.

'Sow the potatoes.' *Thunk*.

'Feed the hens.' *Thunk*.

'Sweep the house, wash the pots, set the dough.' *Thunk*.

'Sleep,' said Freya. She closed her eyes, and leaned on the axe. She wanted nothing more.

7

Gran

Saintly Gran sat with her supper bowl on her knee, in her rocking chair by the fire. She pushed her shoes off. They'd become stiff and uncomfortable with their new rope soles. She did think Freya might have bought her a new pair, as she'd promised.

'But a poor old lady like me isn't worth new shoes,' she said to herself. 'I expect she's got better things to do with her money. She'll want to fritter it away on treats and fancies.'

The fire was getting low. To Gran's weak eyes it was a dim red blur surrounded by shadow. She pulled her shawl tighter round her. Freya was taking her time bringing the wood in. But no doubt Freya had more important things to do than keep an old lady warm.

'If I should freeze, I won't complain,' said Gran. 'It's only the way of the world. The old ones get forgotten, no matter what they've suffered, no matter what they've sacrificed.' She rocked her chair restlessly.

'Buried under tons of earth, at the bottom of the

palace,' she muttered. 'Alone and friendless, trapped in the terrible dungeons of the Sorcerer. Never to return.'

Such an old tale, and she'd told it so many times. It was wearing thin in the telling. The words left a sour taste in her mouth, like curdled milk. She was no longer sure if she wanted them to be true.

A draught blew round her, bringing a smell of wet grass and chicken feed. Freya was back at last, a ripple in the blurred patchwork of Gran's world.

The fire brightened. Freya came close and mouthed unheard words.

'You took so long, I thought I'd better eat my supper before it was quite cold,' Gran retorted. 'No, you have the rest, Freya. I don't care for beans and cabbage. I don't know why you insisted on them so . . . But I don't complain. An old lady like me doesn't need much. *You* finish it off. Don't save any for that lazy Holman.'

She thought Freya shook her head. Was she eating? Gran couldn't tell. She'd cooked the beans and cabbage herself. Cooking was her main task now. She could do it by touch, and if the odd slug or stone went in the pot, what else could be expected of a poor near-blind old lady?

If Freya wanted fancy cooking she would have to do it herself, thought Gran. Then she would be in the house, what's more, giving her lonely old gran some company.

'Stay and talk,' she said. 'I've had no one to talk to for so long. I miss your mother. My poor little girl. Of course you don't remember her, Freya – she died when you were born. Not your fault, I suppose. Such a frail thing she was, just like me. Why she chose your father I'll never understand. He never earned any money, did he?

'And once my poor flower died, your father never took the time to stop and talk to an old lady. Always chasing round the farm, he was. Rushing here, rushing there. Then when the silly man went and got himself drowned – why, Freya, you're not going out again, are you?'

A breeze sprang through the open door.

'You stay here, Freya,' urged Gran. 'You've been out of the house since dawn. You're as bad as your father. Can't Holman do more? What do we pay him for, after all? Tell him to do it. And then you could spend more time inside with your poor old—'

She felt the door slam shut.

'Well!' said Gran, and then remembered that she was a saint. 'Poor girl. No wonder she doesn't want to stop and sit with me. I'm no fit company for anyone, after all. It's my just deserts. I'm just a useless unwanted old lady that nobody loves and nobody cares for. But I don't complain. No, I won't complain.'

And she reached for the abandoned supper bowl, and stretched out her feet to the fire.

8

Gamaran

'Who are you?' said Rab jealously. 'This is *my* dungeon.'
The demon's flash had jolted him fully awake. The
footprints were forgotten as he eyed his companion
with suspicion. He had wanted company, but not just
any old company.

The new prisoner wasn't much older than Rab. He
had dark spiky hair and a thoughtful expression. He
stood up gingerly and shook each limb in turn before
folding up his blanket. His limbs were long, and loose,
and rather clumsy.

'Ouch,' he said. 'Just bruised, I think.' He raised his
head and gazed around appreciatively. 'Mm, nice
dungeon! Plenty of room in here.'

'There *was*,' said Rab pointedly. He decided there was
no need to explain that it was actually a potato cellar.

'There were eight of us in my old dungeon in the
end. It got a bit overcrowded, so they moved me out.
What time do we get fed?'

'In a few hours.' Glumly Rab wondered if they would

get double portions, or if he would have to share. 'Do you want that blanket?' he demanded.

'Please. Be my guest,' said the newcomer politely. He passed the blanket over and sat down, shuffling on the flagstones in a pointless attempt to make himself comfortable.

'So!' he said. 'What did *you* do, to end up here?'

'I defied the Sorcerer,' said Rab coolly. 'I went up to his tower and told him exactly what I thought of him.'

'Goodness!' said the other boy, impressed. 'I shouldn't think he liked that much.'

'He certainly didn't. He seethed with rage. He was speechless with anger.'

'I'll bet! What happened next?'

'He filled the room with spells and purple smoke and made his statues come alive to protect him.'

'Wow! Scary!'

'So I challenged him to a duel.'

'A duel!' The boy's eyes widened. 'What did you fight him with?'

'I had a sword. I was getting the better of him, but he lost his nerve and called up his demons at the last minute,' said Rab. 'He's as mad as a barrelful of hatters. What about you? What did you do?'

'Me? Nothing so heroic,' said the other boy ruefully. 'I'm just a crossword compiler. Crosswords are against the law now. Rule Number 329.'

Rab's lip curled. 'I've never had much time for crosswords. I've had more important things to do . . . So what's your name?'

'Gamaran.'

'Funny sort of name,' said Rab distrustfully.

'It's an anagram.'

'What of?'

'Anagram.'

'Yes, but what *of*?'

'*Anagram!*'*

Rab gave up. He shook his head, and slumped back against the wall. Nothing was turning out as he had hoped. Just his luck, to have to share his dungeon with an idiot.

*Anagram: any word that can be made into a different word (like Gamaran) by shuffling the letters around.

9

Others

Gamaran dozed, too chilly to sleep properly, lulling himself as usual with crossword clues. Letters in small squares drifted gently through his head.

He might have failed as a poet, but at least he could compose crosswords. He wasn't bad at those. Moreover, he'd found everything much easier to cope with once it was reduced to *all in her tiny veg*, 10 letters.*

He yawned, and stretched.

Somebody else yawned, directly opposite.

And someone *else* was snoring, very loudly, next to him. Gamaran opened one eye. The muddy morning light sank into the dungeon like slime in a swamp.

'Three more prisoners!' he observed. 'The dungeons must be getting crowded.'

Then he frowned. Did the old man leaning against the far wall really have only one leg? Surely that wasn't a genuine witch's hat the lady opposite was wearing?

And why did the person lying next to him, snoring

loudly under the blanket, smell so strongly of pig?

The blanket wheezed, rose from the floor, and slid off a smallish pink and grey pig. A grimy hand reached out and grabbed the blanket. The hand's owner, a girl with shaggy black hair and a dirty face, sat up, sniffed, and glared at Gamaran with sullen eyes.

'Good morning, young sir,' the old man said. He had a face full of fierce, cheerful wrinkles, a thick grey beard, and a head as smooth and bald as driftwood. Just as Gamaran thought, he only had one leg. Producing a wooden leg from behind his back, he began to strap it onto his knee. 'Silas, retired buccaneer of the high seas, at your service.'

'Gamaran, at yours.'

'You're a pirate?' asked Rab, incredulously.

'I turned to piracy when I lost my leg to a shark,' said Silas. 'There aren't many jobs open to a one-legged sailor.'

'So are wooden legs against the Rules now?' asked Gamaran curiously.

'Bless you, no, young sir. Not yet, anyway. Sea shanties were my undoing. I just couldn't get out of the habit of singing. Breakfast, anyone?' Silas hobbled over to the hatch, where breakfast was arriving. 'Dry bread, Tulip? This is Tulip Pennywort, licensed witch.'

Gamaran smiled at the old lady very politely, since Rab seemed to be sulking.

'What did you do wrong?' he asked her. 'Was it your spells?'

'Ooh, you wouldn't want to know, dear.' The witch

was very small and spruce in her neat black gown and her tall, pointed hat, as twisted as a tornado. Cackling wickedly, she took up her knitting needles. She was knitting something with a great many sleeves, each as black and slithery as an old banana.

'A little gift for my familiar,' she explained with bright eyes and a crooked smile.

'How nice,' said Gamaran, glancing around uneasily.

'Don't worry, dear, my familiar's safely back at home. Mind, he'd feel quite at home in a dungeon! But that's spiders for you!'

'And the pig?' Rab grumbled crossly. He felt warmer and stronger now: strong enough to resent his cell's new occupants. Not one of them looked fit to be a hero's companion. 'What's the pig been doing to upset the Sorcerer? Singing? Dancing? Playing the tin whistle?'

At this the black-haired girl spoke up sullenly. 'She refused to be the royal bacon. At least, I refused on her behalf.'

'Bacon's forbidden,' said Rab.

'Exactly! That's what *I* said,' she replied. 'The stupid Sorcerer should at least follow his own stupid Rules.'

'Did you say that to Tarcorax?' asked Gamaran in awe.

'Don't be daft! I said it to his cook. I'm only the pig-girl. I'm Swinula.'

'*Swinula?*' sneered Rab.

'I can't help it. It goes with the job.'

Rab scowled. 'You're filthy!'

She pulled a face. 'Well, I live in a pigsty, don't I? Or I used to before I got chucked in here.'

'I don't want a pig in my dungeon!' complained Rab. 'It smells!'

'Only of pig. Anyway, you smell too.'

'At least I don't smell of pig!'

'I'm *proud* to smell of pig,' said Swinula, glowering at Rab. 'Pigs are better people than most people are. Anyway, it's not much of a dungeon. What are all those mouldy potatoes doing here?'

'We had a nice little dungeon of our own,' said the witch reflectively. 'Just me on my own at first, till Silas joined me, then madam and her pig. The dungeons must really be filling up by now! Say thirty cells, six occupants each...' She began to count on her fingers.

'What about you two lads?' asked Silas heartily. 'What brought you here?'

'Crosswords,' replied Gamaran with regret, wishing he could have answered poetry.

'Nothing like a good crossword,' said Tulip. 'I always buy a crossword at the market, and do it with my morning cup of t—. Cup of brimstone.'

'And Rab fought a duel with the Sorcerer,' added Gamaran helpfully, in case Rab was too modest to mention it himself.

'A duel? Ho, yes?' jeered the pig-girl. 'So who won that, then? Give him a good thrashing, did you?'

Gamaran wasn't quite clear who started the fight. Rab yelled something rude at the pig-girl, at which the pig charged and bit him smartly on the ankle. Then when Rab grabbed it by the ears, Swinula leaped to its defence and kicked him in the shins repeatedly, until Silas took off his wooden leg and threatened everybody with it.

'Avast, you mutinous rabble!' he roared. '*And* you, pig!'

'Heel, Porphyry,' said Swinula reluctantly. 'Good girl.' She stroked the pig's ears.

'If I was the Sorcerer,' said Rab, glaring at her, 'I'd eat bacon twice a day.'

'To keep up your strength for all those duels, I suppose?'

Gamaran stepped between them and said hastily, 'Never mind that. It doesn't matter how we got here. We're here now. What I want to know is, why? Why are the dungeons full? What's going on? Why is the Sorcerer doing this to us?'

'Because he's mad,' Rab answered sulkily.

'Yes, but why? What drove him to it?'

The witch waved her knitting in the air triumphantly. '*I* know,' she said.

---

* Answer: everything (anagram of 'her tiny veg')

10

Reason

'It was his daughter,' said Tulip.

'His daughter drove him mad?'

'Only in a manner of speaking. Hopping mad, that's for sure.'

'But how?'

'He lost her, that's how.'

'You mean she died?'

The witch hesitated.

'He killed her, so the rumour goes,' said Silas, his voice low. 'They say there's a fresh grave in the palace gardens.'

'I heard he imprisoned her in his highest tower,' said Swinula. 'Without a stair.'

'Let *me* tell it!' The witch pushed her tangle of knitting to one side, and straightened her corkscrew of a hat. 'Now then. Tarcorax has – or had – a daughter. Amaranth, she was called, and from all accounts she was the spitting image of her father, minus the beard and eyebrows of course. Red hair down to her waist, vain as a peacock. Always strutting around in silk dresses, the works.'

'So was she beautiful?' asked Swinula scornfully, tossing back her grubby tangle of black hair.

'Oh, I dare say. Princesses always are. But her temper! She was like the Sorcerer in that as well. Wilful! You wouldn't believe it. Stubborn and pig-headed, that's what she was.'

'Nothing wrong with that,' sniffed Swinula, patting Porphyry's nose.

'But what happened?' begged Gamaran.

'They had a row, and he disowned her, that's what!'

'I heard it was the other way around,' said Silas.

'Will you stop interrupting me! As I was saying. They had a row – an almighty, thunderous row. It could be heard throughout the palace. Sparks flew. Windows broke. Chairs exploded.'

'What?'

'Well, something like that, anyway. I didn't actually see it myself,' explained Tulip.

'It wasn't *chairs*, it was his *throne*,' said Swinula.

'And how would you know, madam?'

'I know a stableboy whose sister is a maid who's married to a footman in the palace,' she answered smugly.

'But what was the row about?' demanded Gamaran. 'What could make him so angry that he turns his country upside down, makes hundreds of Rules, and throws half his people into prison?'

'Well, that I don't know. Perhaps the expert can tell

us?' Tulip glared at Swinula, who shrugged.

'What I do know is this,' the witch went on. 'Since that argument, no one has set eyes on Amaranth. She's vanished; no one knows where. Some say he killed her in his anger. Others say he's locked her in a secret corner of the palace, and surrounded her with spells to keep her hidden. Who knows? Only Tarcorax. Anyway, that was the start of the trouble. Since then, he's made more and madder Rules every day.'

Rab had been listening intently. 'If he killed her, she must be avenged,' he said.

'By you?' asked the pig-girl with a sneer.

'Why not? I come from a family of heroes,' he answered haughtily. 'My grandpa died in these very dungeons, trying to tunnel his way out.'

'Did he indeed!' said Silas, looking startled.

'Surely the Sorcerer wouldn't kill his own daughter,' objected Gamaran. 'She's more likely in a dungeon just like us.'

Tulip shook her head. 'He wouldn't keep her in a common dungeon.'

'Highest tower, like I said,' insisted Swinula.

A princess in trouble! New, bright images flickered through Rab's head. Pale hands beseeching him from a topmost window, a pair of helpless and imploring eyes behind a veil of flame-gold hair: a daring rescue, a royal hand in marriage, half a kingdom won...

'If he's hidden her,' he said decisively, 'she must be found.' *This* was his task, his destiny. He was ready to start.

45

'How?' asked Gamaran with interest.

Rab turned to Tulip. 'You're a licensed witch—'

'Licensed to charm warts,' muttered Swinula.

'–so why can't you cast a spell to find Amaranth?'

The witch screwed up her eyes. 'Ah. Well, you see, that's difficult.'

'Why?' demanded Swinula. 'It's only a finding spell. Surely that's not too hard for you?'

'Not at all! I meant it's dangerous,' explained the witch. 'Not for *me*, of course. But it might be dangerous for bystanders.'

'All right,' said Rab. 'If finding the princess is too difficult and dangerous – how about something nice and easy to start with, like getting us out of here?'

11

Tarcorax

Tarcorax sat lost in thought upon his throne of glass, which was held together in a makeshift way with sticky tape and bandages. His hand rested on a fat, musty book entitled *Spells of Concealment*. The glass gryphon, Hieronymus, sat beside him like a patient dog that has given up all expectation of going out for a walk.

I hate this palace, thought Tarcorax. It's too big. Too cold. Too bright. *Glass*, of all things...It never wears out, that's the worst of it. I'm stuck with it. I can't pull it down, because my great-great-goodness-knows-how-many-greats grandfather built it. It's tradition. It's sacred. Anyway, it's protected with so many spells I probably couldn't knock it down if I tried.

'He must have been mad,' said Tarcorax aloud.

After a moment, Hieronymus asked carefully,
'Who?'

'Tarcorax the first, of course. Why *glass*? I know, I know – he wanted to see everything that was going on, inside the palace and out. But I can't stand it. I don't *want* to see out there, all that ragtag and riffraff milling around. And I certainly don't want *them* seeing *in.*'

He strode over to the wall and twitched aside one of the heavy tapestries. A spear of icy, dazzling daylight lanced across the room. A glass falcon fell from its perch with a crash at the shock.

Tarcorax screwed up his eyes against the glare and squinted out. Averting his gaze from the garden far below, he stared at the marketplace. As usual, there was nothing of interest there, just little people scurrying around mindlessly like insects...busy complaining about the Rules, no doubt.

'Hah!' he barked. 'They don't know how lucky they've been. I was too soft on them. But they're going to take some notice of me now! You're all going to obey me now, or else. D'you hear?'

'I hear you, Master. I obey,' the gryphon offered anxiously.

'Of course you do! I created you! I wish I could remake that rabble out there; melt them down and mould them anew. My dungeons shall do it for me,' muttered Tarcorax. 'If they don't like it, that's *her* fault.'

She'd turned up her nose at his spells. He grew cold with anger at the memory.

She'd laughed at his demons. She'd mocked his familiar, the glass gryphon. Perhaps a glass familiar was a bad idea, but that was beside the point...She shouldn't have laughed at him.

Above him, the air began to fizz. A demon appeared,

shedding orange sparks on the floor, and smiled at him sidelong.

'They're full,' it blurted out.

'What are?'

'Dungeons. All full up. Even the potato cellar. We *told* you.'

'So what do you expect me to do about it?' enquired the Sorcerer coldly.

'Erm . . .' The demon shrugged and fiddled with the end of its tail.

'Squeeze them in,' snarled Tarcorax. 'Use a shoehorn if you have to. I don't care.'

The demon faltered. 'Food's a bit short. They take a lot of feeding.'

'Cut their rations.'

'Humans are nothing to me, Master,' said the demon, squirming, 'but don't you think – erm—'

'Yes?'

'Well, some of them aren't very well.'

'So?'

'Some of them are quite old.'

'So?'

'You're not making yourself very popular,' said the demon.

'By all the celestial bodies, let us salute the astounding cleverness of this demon!'

The demon tried a grin, and thought better of it.

'Let us marvel at its unparalleled powers of observation! For it has noticed that I am NOT VERY POPULAR!'

'Not very,' said the demon uneasily.

'I do not WANT to be popular!' bellowed Tarcorax. 'I will be the most unpopular sovereign this land has ever SEEN before I'm through!'

'Yes, Master,' said the unhappy demon. 'So, erm, what shall I do about the rumours, then?'

'Rumours?'

The demon cleared its throat and mumbled, 'The – ahem – you know, sort of, um, buried in the garden.'

'Nothing but clothes,' said Tarcorax, his voice like steel. 'Clothes prove nothing. If anyone says otherwise, they go straight into the dungeons with the rest.'

'But—'

'On bread and water! Now GO AWAY!'

'That's all they're getting anyhow,' sniffed the demon as it vanished.

Tarcorax slumped back upon his throne, ignoring the creaking of bandages. The glass gryphon edged forward until it could place a transparent paw on the Sorcerer's foot; but Tarcorax saw nothing, felt nothing, but his own bitterness.

12

Magic

'Not even magic can find a way out of here,' said the witch sulkily. 'These dungeons are the oldest part of the palace, and the strongest. There are spells woven into their walls.'

'Have you tried?'

She glared at Rab. 'I tell you, it can't be done!'

'Well, *I'm* not giving up so easily!' said Rab. 'Surely a glass ceiling can't be all that hard to break! Silas? Lend us your leg.'

Silas unstrapped his wooden leg. Climbing on Gamaran's shoulders, Rab whacked at the ceiling with it.

'Oy!' protested Silas. 'Don't batter it so hard. I'll get splinters!'

'Not even a dent,' said Rab, disgusted. He dropped the leg. 'Knitting needle!' Tulip handed up a needle which Rab poked into the corners of the ceiling, prising at the biggest cracks in the murky glass. Nothing happened, except a shower of spiders.

'Harder than I thought,' he panted.

'I told you!' said Tulip. 'You haven't got a hope. It'd take very strong magic indeed to break out of these dungeons. They're indestructible. Now give me back my needle.'

Rab held it behind his back. 'Not unless you help us. There must be some spell you can do – *some* magic you can work! Call yourself a witch? Even if you can't get us out of here, do *something*!'

'What sort of something?'

'Something to make Tarcorax sit up and take notice!'

Swinula was looking thoughtful. 'I know how we could stir him up a bit,' she said.

'Is that a good idea?' asked Silas doubtfully.

'Why not?' said Rab. 'He's already thrown us in the dungeons. What else can he do to us?'

'Quite a lot, actually,' said Silas with a shudder, but the pig-girl paid him no attention.

'You're right!' she told Rab. 'We don't have to obey his precious Rules any more! Why should we? He's done his worst. We can forget all that stupid business about No singing – No playing – No joking – No pets—'

'No parties,' said Rab gloomily.

'No poetry,' sighed Gamaran.

'No dancing,' murmured Silas.

'No frilly frocks,' said Tulip wistfully, and then pulled herself together. 'That's all very well, but we could sing and dance till we were blue in the face down here, and it wouldn't do *him* any harm.'

'I'm not talking about singing and dancing,' said

52

Swinula. 'I'm talking about magic. Your magic. I think you should delete the Rules.'

'Yes! Wipe them clean off the walls!' said Rab excitedly. 'Paint over them, pull them down, make them invisible. That'll really annoy Tarcorax!'

Swinula gave him a pitying look. 'I mean more than wipe them off the walls. I mean delete them, destroy them, wipe them out of existence.'

Tulip looked alarmed. 'What, all of them? All at once?'

'Just one would do, to start with. Deleting one little law from the lists shouldn't be difficult, should it, for a witch of your calibre?' Swinula gave Tulip a smile like a shark.

'Which one?' said Tulip faintly.

'Any. Whichever's easiest.'

'Come on, Tulip! It's worth a go,' suggested Silas.

'You've got to do it!' entreated Rab.

'You're our only hope,' persuaded Swinula.

'It would be nice to have poetry back,' sighed Gamaran.

Tulip looked from face to eager face, then dropped her gaze to her knitting. Carefully she rolled up its eight black sleeves (which were all of different lengths), and stuck her remaining needle through it.

'Very well,' she said resignedly. 'I suppose I'll have to try.'

13

Tulip

It's been such a long time, thought Tulip Pennywort. It must be twenty years since I last did a proper spell. But I can't tell them that I got thrown into the dungeons for flower-arranging – not when they're all relying on me like this.

Serves me right for showing off. Trying to impress them with the knitting, when Cranford's really only as big as my hand. I suppose I can always use it to keep the draughts off his web . . . if I ever get out of here, that is.

The faces were all turned to her expectantly. Tulip sighed and racked her brains.

She *had* known some spells, once upon a time, when she was young and still had ambitions to be a proper witch, before she realised that a good stern glare worked as well as many a magic charm . . .

Now which spell had she been best at? She cast her mind back. She'd never mastered invisibility – her shape-shifting had always been a bit dodgy – but she had to do *something*.

Just have a go, Tulip told herself. If I can get started, maybe it'll come back to me. All I need is a simple little transformation spell, after all. Nothing major. She took a deep breath, raised her hands to the ceiling, stretched her fingers, and intoned:

'ALACAZAR! ADAMANTAR! MARANTOR!'

Then she turned three times widdershins, to give herself time to think. The old water-into-tar spell was coming back to her now; or was it the stone-into-frog?

Whatever it was, it would have to do.

'By Toadflax, Baneberry, and Stinking Hellebore,' said the witch, and got stuck. She took another deep breath and thought of her window box. 'By knotweed and parsley, by sneezewort and geranium, *Mazri, Dazri, Alacazoo!'*

Everyone was still looking at her hopefully, and nothing was happening. She needed something more: but her mind had gone blank. She couldn't recall a single spell. All she could think of was her knitting pattern.

'Purl one, yarn forward, cable two from the back, slip one, knit one, knit two together,' gabbled the witch.

All at once the temperature dropped. The dungeon began to mist before her eyes.

'Purl five make one?'

The mist thickened and swirled as if the flagstones were on fire. Porphyry squealed in alarm as pillars of smoke twined up towards the ceiling.

'Knit one, slip one, yarn forward twice!' cried the witch triumphantly.

There was a dazzling flash and a deafening bang. The smoke dissolved away.

14

Rhyme

Silas rubbed his eyes. 'What's she done? Was that a gun?'

Gamaran said dreamily, 'I liked that swirly sort of cloud, but the bang was rather loud.'

Rab turned impatiently to the witch. 'Mist and smoke's all very well, but what exactly *was* that spell?'

'It must have been strong, to produce all that murk,' said Gamaran. 'Tell us how long it'll take to work—' He stopped short, with a startled expression.

The pig-girl, catching Porphyry up in her arms, began to gasp with amazed laughter. Tears trickled from her eyes.

'If you ask me—' said Silas. He shook his head. 'I'm all at sea.'

Tulip opened her mouth, and closed it again without saying anything.

Gamaran spoke to nobody in particular, listening to his own words as carefully as if someone else was saying them.

'Is this some kind of weird curse?
I find my words come out in verse.
When I try not to rhyme, like now,
The rhymes just pop out anyhow!
And I can't help it – even when
I try to stop, I rhyme. Like then.'

Wiping her eyes, Swinula asked him:

'Why should you sound so appalled?
You wanted verse to be recalled.
Here's your chance to have a go at
Being the world's first non-stop poet!'

'But it's not *me* rhyming, is it?'
'Who cares? I think you sound exquisite.'
Rab put in fiercely,

'That is *not* the point. Here, you!
Just what are you trying to do?'

He jumped up and jabbed an angry finger at the
witch, who recoiled. Before she could reply, Swinula
came to her defence.

'What's your problem? Why the panic?
There's no need to be volcanic.
She's cast her spell without a flaw,
And just repealed the seventh law.'

'That's right,' squeaked the witch, and found herself adding, 'Good night!'

> 'Well, I don't *want* to talk in verse!
> I'm sure that nothing could be worse,'

fumed Rab. Swinula raised her eyebrows in exasperation.

> 'Just calm down and stop your squealing.
> Imagine how the wizard's feeling!
> If it's annoying *you*, well then,
> It must be bugging *him* times ten!'

Silas said in a small voice, 'I don't mind confessing, I find this depressing.'
'Then so will he, to a greater degree!' The pig-girl grinned exultantly.

> 'I'll bet he's well and truly vexed!
> Which law should Tulip strike out next?'

Gamaran had fallen completely silent. He had tried to write poetry for so long, with such great effort and heartache, and so little success. Now the gift was handed out to everyone. Ruefully he thought:

> If I'm a poet, who would know it?

15

Hieronymus

Since glass gryphons seldom speak, Hieronymus was not
badly affected by the poetry. However, he had to watch
his angry master striding up and down the room, slashing
at ancient tapestries with his sword, sweeping ornaments
aside in crashing showers of glass, and spluttering as he
tried to say his spells.

None of them would work. They turned into sonnets
and quatrains instead.

As Tarcorax stamped back and forth in strangled fury,
Hieronymus followed three paces behind. He placed his
feet delicately. Creatures made of glass need to be careful
how they tread. Hieronymus knew that he looked
fearsome; he also knew that he was fragile. His feet tinkled
slightly in their cautious pursuit of the Sorcerer.

Tarcorax whirled on him irritably.

'Oh, stop it! Now, hop it!'

The gryphon, who could not hop without breaking his
ankles, felt his way backwards as gingerly as a cat, and sat
back on his haunches, dolefully watching his beloved
master.

The Sorcerer gave up trying to utter spells. He swore viciously, in rhyme, and stabbed at the dead fire with the point of his staff. Dragging it through the cold ashes, he wove a pattern of lines: an endless knot. Blue grey it glowed, then green, then burned to orange; then sighed and faded back to grey. Tarcorax fretted.

'I don't understand! Where in my land lies the power to do this? How could I miss a magic so strong? Something's wrong, something's wrong!'

The gryphon shrank back from the glowing ashes. He was terrified of magic. Magic had brought him to life; only magic could kill him. In the meantime, he was as brittle as a dead leaf, with wings that were as useless as they were beautiful, and magic did nothing to help him about *that*.

He hated the way magic crackled and fizzled and spat. He disliked the demons who now bounded, glittering and grimacing, from the air. Show-offs, thought Hieronymus. Posers.

Tarcorax thundered at them.

'Find me the source of this new power, and bring him here – within the hour!' The demons nodded, winked, and disappeared.

New shapes were emerging from the dead fire. Like the shadows of caterpillars, they started to crawl slowly across the floor, twine around the legs of the glass statues, and slither up the walls.

Hieronymus, shuddering, withdrew to the far side of the tower. He made for the picture that was turned to the wall, its plain brown back facing outward, and crept behind it. There he hid, wedged between a musty tapestry and the portrait of his master's disgraced daughter. Her painted face stared into the darkness.

Hieronymus lay down beside her. He had been both fond and afraid of Amaranth, though not as fond and afraid as he was of his master.

He thought back to the dreadful day when everything had altered. The two of them had always argued, but the last argument had been the worst.

'You can't make me wear *that*,' Amaranth had said in a voice full of horror and disgust.

'You'll wear what I tell you,' said Tarcorax grimly.

'I'll wear what I like, and I'll do what I like!'

'You've done what you like for too long! I've been too lenient.' Tarcorax spoke through gritted teeth. 'I've let you run wild. Yesterday you came to dinner two hours late and soaking wet!'

'I was hunting frogs,' said Amaranth.

'Looking for a frog-prince to marry?' said Tarcorax scornfully.

'Who said anything about princes?' Amaranth lifted her chin and tossed back her mane of fiery hair. 'Who cares about princes and palaces and all that royal rubbish? I can hunt frogs if I want to.'

'What about your magic studies, pray?'

'Frogs are more interesting.'

'For goodness' sake, Amaranth, you're a princess! And one day you will be Queen, though heaven help this country when you are, since as far as I can see you have no more interest or talent in magic than a peasant. I should have made you buckle down and study magic years ago!'

'Made me?' said Amaranth coldly. 'You think you could have *made* me?' At this point Hieronymus had begun to creep backwards, out of the way.

'You are my daughter,' growled Tarcorax, 'and you'll do as I command. You must learn the magic arts!'

'Must?' asked the princess. '*Must*?'

'*Must!*' Tarcorax bellowed in frustration, his cheeks reddening. 'Look around you! For generations your ancestors have reigned from this historic tower! You will rule a great and noble realm—'

'Great? Noble?' mocked Amaranth. 'Who do *you* rule? You don't care about your people, and they don't care about you! All you care about are spells. So just tell me, Father, who takes the slightest notice of your rules?'

'Sorcerers need magic, and you will be the next Sorcerer!' roared Tarcorax. The gryphon, catching a glimpse of his furious face, had closed his eyes quickly. 'Yet you refuse to learn even the simplest spell!'

'I don't give tuppence for your magic. I didn't *ask* to be your heir.'

'I suppose you'd rather be a – a fishmonger's daughter? One of the rabble out there? A nobody?' shouted Tarcorax.

'Yes,' said Amaranth deliberately. 'Yes, since you ask. I would rather be nobody.'

Silence fell. Half the candles went out.

'Then beware,' said the Sorcerer very quietly, 'lest nobody is exactly what you become.'

At that point Hieronymus had folded his wings around his head, afraid of what else he might hear. Even so, he could not block out the terrible crash and scream that followed. When he dared to look up, the Sorcerer's throne was in pieces; and the princess was gone.

'An accident,' said Tarcorax, kicking the splintered pieces of throne aside. His voice was hoarse. His face was wet. Hieronymus asked no questions. He had not seen Amaranth since.

Two days later, the first new list of Rules had gone up on the palace gates. Soon after that, the dungeons had begun to fill.

Now, from his dark shelter behind the portrait, Hieronymus heard the fizz and crackle of the demons' return. He poked his head out, curious to see the cause of all the poetry.

However, the demons were empty-handed. They spoke with quick shrugs, and embarrassed sideways leers.

'Couldn't find him. Couldn't track him down.'

Tarcorax froze, staring at them. His bushy red eyebrows drew together.

'Speak again!' he commanded.

'Can't find him, whoever he is doing the magic. S-sorry,' stuttered the demons. 'Too well-shielded. There's no trail.'

The Sorcerer continued to gaze at them for a long, silent moment, while they writhed. Steam began to rise from them. They wanted to be gone.

'Never mind,' said the Sorcerer at last, almost absent-mindedly. 'Go away. It doesn't matter now.'

16

Mist

Freya hadn't said a word all day, having nobody but Gran to say it to; so the poetry came and went unnoticed. Perhaps Gran's chatter sounded a little different from usual, but Freya was too busy to actually listen to any of it. She knew it by heart anyway: poor old lady, what a burden I am, won't complain, and what about a cup of tea?

Freya had no time to spend on thoughts of Gran. She was thinking about cows.

One was sick, one was lame, one was due to calve. And she still hadn't mended the walls. She needed more chicken feed (but how could she pay for it?), they were nearly out of firewood again and she'd wrenched her shoulder trying to catch an angry sheep.

She made no time to think about Rab either. When the thought stole upon her, questioning where Rab might be, she felt sick with fear and hatred. Gone like the grandpa she couldn't remember, gone like the father she couldn't forget . . . She shut the thought away.

The day was too short for all that had to be done. It was past midnight when Freya fell upon her bed, Gran snoring beside her. Five hours later she dragged herself up again, with bleary eyes and a dry mouth, to start the morning chores.

It was the hour before dawn. The faded world was quiet, resting before the day's arrival. The fields lay shrouded in grey dreams. Down in the valley, the river was hidden by a long bank of mist, pale and fathomless.

Freya stopped with the bucket in her hand to gaze at the drift of river mist. It was as soft and spotless as a new feather quilt. If she were to walk down under its peaceful covering, she thought, nothing would matter any more. Her troubles would no longer exist. She could rest there for ever.

The idea caught at her. She did so want to rest . . .

The bucket fell from her grasp. She took three long strides down the hill towards the river and its beckoning blanket. Then a sheep dashed up and butted her full in the stomach.

Freya sat down with a thump, winded and gasping. The sheep had its sharp hooves on her chest and was trying to lick her face.

'Get off! Shoo!' said Freya, struggling to her feet. The sheep fell back, but only for a moment. It jumped up repeatedly, like an eager dog leaping at its master. Freya caught it by its fleece and firmly set it down again.

But here came another one, bouncing towards her as

excited as a spring lamb, and it would have leapt up exactly like the first if Freya hadn't side-stepped it.

'What on earth...?' exclaimed Freya, and then the cows arrived, Daisy, Maisie and Wallop, all galloping towards her in extraordinary haste, with lame old Clover trying to keep up behind. They brushed against Freya lovingly, almost squashing her between their huge, warm bodies, and gave her rasping licks with their long tongues. Even Wallop, named for the fearsome power of her kick, was unnaturally and alarmingly affectionate.

'Yes, yes, I love you too,' said a bewildered Freya, 'but it's nearly milking time! You should be in the cow shed.' She had to walk to the cow shed with all four of them jostling to be next to her, and puffing in her ear.

No sooner had Freya persuaded the cows into their stalls than the five farm cats came stalking out of the hay to twine themselves around her legs, purring like a whole hive of bees. Then Nab the cantankerous old sheepdog ambled up, laid his nose upon her foot, and gazed at her beseechingly.

'Not you as well!' said Freya. 'What *is* the matter with everyone? At least there can't be any more – oh, no!'

From the darkest corners of the cow shed, rats came creeping, scuttling towards her. The cats turned to hiss at them jealously. A pair of swallows swooped round Freya's head. She flapped them away, and found a sleepy bat trying to nestle in her hair.

That was the last straw. She'd had enough. She

backed swiftly out of the cow shed, bolting the door behind her.

But already a flock of field mice was rustling to her heels; a molehill began to tumble open at her feet, and a cloud of butterflies alighted on her arms, as if they'd mistaken her for a bushful of blossom.

Freya was simply exasperated. 'How can I milk the cows,' she said, trying vainly to brush the butterflies away, 'how can I get anything done, with all *this* going on?'

17

Pets

'But I don't *want* to make friends with a rat!'

'It's traditional,' Gamaran assured Rab. 'Prisoners in dungeons always do it. Anyway, it doesn't look as though you have a choice.'

Rab glowered at the sleek black rat, which sat up on its haunches gazing at him with rapturous devotion.

'This is your fault,' he complained to Tulip. She was hunched in a corner, trying to ignore the two adoring toads that were hopping closer and closer.

'Don't blame me,' she whined. 'I only meant pets should be *allowed*. I didn't mean they should be compulsory.'

'Tell that to the rat! You got the spell wrong this time, didn't you?' snapped Rab. 'Oh, go away.' He aimed a kick at the rat. It slunk away reproachfully and began sidling up to Gamaran instead.

'Whoever would have thought there was so much wildlife in a dungeon?' asked Silas, warily observing a company of slugs making their treacly way towards him. 'Get away, there. Whoa, whoa! *Sit!* Oh, damn.'

'I can't stand it,' groaned Rab. 'I wish I was back home. I'm sure this sort of thing never happened to Grandpa!' He picked a giant centipede off his leg and flung it at the wall.

Swinula hugged her pig, bright-eyed. 'Pets! You've all got pets! Porphyry, no one will ever dare laugh at you again.' Porphyry snuffled at a beetle that was wandering across the floor in search of an owner, and crunched it up enthusiastically.

'Next time,' said Rab, scowling at Tulip, 'pick something that doesn't involve rats! How about deleting the Rule on puddings? That should be harmless enough. Or flags, or toys, or gardens!'

'Gardens?' said Tulip, perking up. 'I know a bit about gardens. I'll think about that one.' She reached out a cautious hand to tickle one of the toads under the chin, which proved to be a mistake. Wiping the slime from her fingers, she began to shuffle through her memory for another knitting pattern. It was amazing how magical the double loop stitch had proved to be.

'But no more pets!' snapped Rab.

Gamaran sneaked his hand into his pocket and gently felt the little ball of fluff that sat hidden there. It was blue, with yellow eyes and seven legs. It had made a beeline for him, although it was not a bee, but a quert. He knew this because he had invented it for a poem when he was younger.

Fur as blue as cloudless skies
And gold as lemons are thy eyes
And fourteen toes of smallest size
Know no evil, do no hurt,
O happy tender tiny Quert!

And now his poem sat in his pocket, snuggling up to his fingers. It made him glow with quiet pride.

'Well, I rather like them,' he said.

18

An Old Tale

Saintly Gran sat by the fire, rocking herself to and fro, to and fro. She neither saw nor heard the mice that scuttled, squeaking for attention, between the rockers of her chair. She was full of worries.

Freya's face loomed suddenly before her, blocking out the firelight. Freya's voice, tiny and distant, fluttered in her ear. Something about bedtime?

'In a while,' said Gran. 'Sit down over there, my dear.'

Freya's face disappeared. Colours shifted and shrank, until Gran presumed she had sat down. Rock, rock, went Gran's chair, shaking up the sorrows in her head until she felt them bubbling and fizzing in her ears, and they had to be let out.

'You're working too hard, Freya,' she said. 'I know it's all my fault. I'm just a useless old woman, a burden to everybody. I don't complain, dear, but I know what you think. You don't want me here, a helpless poor old lady.'

The colours that were Freya moved again, then were still.

Rock, rock, went Gran's chair. 'I know about Rab, as well,' she mourned. 'My dear, brave, foolish boy! What a hero he is! You don't need to tell me where he's gone – I know it all. Just like his grandpa before him, he's gone to the palace, poor boy. And like his grandpa, he won't come back. All for his old gran's sake – all because of me.'

Faster and faster she rocked, until her worst sorrow finally came bursting out, the words tumbling over themselves in their hurry to be said.

'Oh, Freya! I have to tell you. It's preying on my mind. I've got a secret. A terrible secret. Your grandpa didn't die, not in the dungeons of the Sorcerer, not at all. I don't know where he is. Your grandpa never went near the Sorcerer. I just told you that because it sounded better than the truth.

'The truth is, he ran away. Away from me. Away from my complaining, so he said.

'Do I complain? Never! Not any more. Perhaps I did, a little, back then when I was young. I wasn't a saint then. I came from a good family, you see; a wonderful house, everything I wanted. Your grandpa said I was as lovely as a lily. He was a fine figure of a man – but he was poor. When I married him, my parents refused to speak to me. They cut me off without a penny, and who can blame them?

'I regretted it myself, soon enough. I hated being a farmer's wife. Oh, the dreadful shabby clothes I had to wear! And the farmhouse was so small and dark, and the work was so hard! I just couldn't do it. I was a dainty young girl, not used to such rough labour.

'And what a great clodhopper your grandpa was, clunking around the house in his dirty big boots! His hands were never clean. And he had no time for me. He never talked to me – spent all his time out with the animals, never a word for me in the evenings. Always busy, busy.

'Well, well. We came from different worlds. Why should he make allowances for a delicate young girl? He should never have married a frail little thing like me.

'For twenty years I put up with it. If I complained, it was with good reason. Our children were born, grown and fled from home, yet still we had no money, no nice things. Wouldn't *you* complain?'

Gran gave Freya long enough to make an unheard assent. Then, dropping her voice, she went on.

'Then I caught the fever. I was terribly ill. He nursed me through it – after his fashion. I had to nag him for a week before he'd sell his precious ram to pay for the best medicine. But I don't complain.' Gran rocked her chair peevishly.

'The fever went, but my eyes began to fail. The best medicine made no difference. I expect your grandpa had been cheated – he was always easily taken in. I begged and begged him to go to the Sorcerer and ask his help. "If anyone can cure me," I would say, "surely the Sorcerer can. Sell the bull," I told him, "offer him half your land. Must I live in shadow all my life?"

'You know what he replied? "Your shadow's nothing, next to mine."'

'I couldn't understand him. "What do you mean?" I said.'

"I'm sick of endless work," he answered, "and I'm even sicker of your endless complaining. I'm going away," he said. And away he went, without another word. Just like that. Leaving me all alone.'

Gran paused, hoping Freya might offer her some touch of comfort. None came. Her shoulders slumped wretchedly.

'And that's what he did,' she murmured at last. 'I've heard nothing from him since. I told everyone he'd gone to meet the Sorcerer and had died in the dungeons. All through the long years, I've told that story. For a long time I wished it was true. Yet now, sometimes, I miss him.'

Gran sighed. The rocking of her chair slowed. The mice sat up and cleaned their whiskers.

'After that, my daughter – your poor mother – moved back in with me, along with her husband and their baby. That was Rab: a noisy, red-faced little thing he was. They tried to run the farm, and a poor cack-handed job they made of it. But did I complain? Not a word!

'Your mother was delicate, just like me. You were the death of her, Freya. I lost her and ended up with you. And a sickly baby you were – not a shouter like your brother; you were a peaky little whimperer. But did I complain? Not I! Even as my ears and eyes grew weaker by the day, I would not complain.

'No. I'm cured of complaining. You've never heard me

complain, have you, Freya? Not when the crops failed and I went hungry. Not when blizzards buried the house, though my old bones ached with the cold. Not even when the river flooded – you remember – and your father drowned, trying to save the sheep.' Gran shook her head. 'Of all the stupid, stubborn men! Why couldn't he leave the sheep to drown instead? But that was your father for you. He left me all alone again. So I hired Holman, and I never complained.

'Now Rab's gone too, my poor, brave boy. You've tried to hide it from me, but I know. He believed all my stories. He's gone to follow his grandpa, hasn't he – gone to beg the Sorcerer for my cure? Hasn't he, Freya?'

Freya neither moved nor spoke. Gran shivered. The truth lay now before her as bare and monstrous as a newborn babe.

'All for my sake,' Gran whispered. 'It's all my fault. I wish I'd never told that tale. It's swollen in the telling, grown teeth and claws and a hungry belly. Will you forgive me, Freya? Can you pardon me for all that's past, for driving away your grandpa, for telling all those tales, for being such a poor old woman, such a burden? Freya, do forgive me.'

Gran felt tears creep down her cheeks. All was still, with such a profound stillness that Gran began to fear she had lost Freya too. Her hands trembled on the arms of her chair.

19

An Older Tale

Hens, thought Freya as soon as she sat down. Damn. I haven't fed the hens.

She could easily slip out unnoticed. Gran had already set off along the well-worn track of what a burden she was, poor old lady, and would be safely stuck in that rut for the next ten minutes.

Leaving her coat on the chair, Freya got up slowly: only quick movements caught Gran's eye. She glided outside. None too soon – Gran was starting on about what a hero Rab was, and Freya wasn't in the mood for that. She *knew* he was a hero. It didn't help.

The cool evening air calmed her down. After a while she stopped hurling handfuls of corn at the startled hens, and realised that the sheep weren't chasing her any more. Now they just ignored her, as normal, and so did nearly all the cows. When Freya walked down to gaze into the river valley, the only animal to follow her was Wallop.

The sun had just set. Yet down in the valley, mist was

already starting to thicken. The whisper of the hidden water crept up to her ears, speaking soft words she couldn't quite make out, as tender as a parent's lullaby. Ever since her father had died in the flood waters, Freya had strained to understand the river's language, but there was no meaning there.

River mist shouldn't form at this time of day, thought Freya. It's not even dark yet. But maybe down there, time is different. Maybe down there it's always the hour before dawn, that strange, quiet hour when nothing yet seems real. The time of rest, of waiting. When there's no one else in all the world ... apart from the Dawn Walker.

She stood like a statue, hand on her chest, heart thumping. Why had the Dawn Walker crept into her mind? He was an old tale, half-forgotten, that no one ever wanted to remember.

But now that she had remembered, Freya could almost feel him down there in the mist, striding, gliding through it on his endless travels, unseen and unheard. Cloaked and hooded, silent as the grave ...

The Dawn Walker. People hardly ever spoke of him. But in a house where somebody lay sick, the older folk would still put holly on their lintels, and a candle in each window, to keep the Dawn Walker away.

And after foggy nights, they said, if you saw his footprints on the grass, then be sure to check them carefully, and pray that they might point to someone else's house, to someone else's grief, and not to yours ...

Wallop mooed loudly in her left ear, making her start.

'Come on, then,' she said. Reluctantly she pulled herself away from the white calm of the river valley, and trudged back up the hill. Gran might soon realise she was gone. So shooing Wallop back towards the pasture, she slid inside the farmhouse. Gran was still talking.

'Poor old woman, such a burden,' Gran was saying. Freya saw that there were tears in her eyes.

'Freya, do forgive me,' quavered Gran. She had ceased to rock. Her old mottled hands trembled on the arms of her chair. Mice scurried away across the floor.

Freya stood on the threshold. She observed the spluttering fire, the greasy pan beneath the hole in the roof, the heap of dirty washing gently stinking in a corner, Gran's bent back, and her wet, wrinkled cheeks.

Walking over to Gran's chair, she took the old hands in her own.

'Don't worry, Gran,' she said as clearly as she could, stroking the gnarled fingers so that Gran would understand. 'There's nothing to forgive. Don't worry. Everything's all right.'

20

Wallop

Inside the house, the lamp went out and all fell quiet.

Outside, in the moonlight, Wallop leaned lovingly against the farmhouse wall. This was the closest she could get to Freya, her little, ungainly, two-legged calf, but as soon as Freya emerged from the house again in the morning, Wallop would be here for her, waiting.

She scratched her side against the windowsill, and nosed around the moonlit path for a quick snack. However, there was no grass, only stones. Wallop's tongue found a single lanky dandelion struggling from a crack in the hard ground.

Never mind, thought Wallop. She would go hungry for her dear Freya's sake. How could she ever have wanted to kick her?

As she pulled at the lonely dandelion, Wallop paused, disconcerted. Another shoot was growing from the crack, uncurling as she watched. Two dark leaves unfolded; a pale bud sought out the moonlight. Wallop put her mouth down to it by instinct, and stopped dead.

This was not right. She should not be able to *see* a plant growing like this! Her eyes rolled in alarm.

In the next crack along, a second shoot slid from the earth. Then another, and another; dark stems twining swiftly, long leaves unfurling into droopy hearts. Soon Wallop was surrounded by plants she dared not eat. She began to trample uneasily to and fro.

The plants were creeping upwards, climbing the farmhouse walls. Their leading shoots nudged at the windows.

My Freya! thought Wallop, and began to moo urgently in warning. The stems caught her legs like nooses; the leaves crowded at her flanks. When she kicked at the strange plants, they tangled tight around her hooves.

Wallop's instinct was to escape. A few yards, and she'd be safe, for the plants were only growing by the house, not in the open ground. Nevertheless, she set her mind on Freya and stayed at her post, breathing hard. She would hold out until the leaves came up to her neck...

They stopped just short of that. Wallop stood, trembling, belly-deep in a sea of dark green hearts. For a short while, all was still. Poised motionless, the plants drank in the moonlight.

Then a white bud slowly raised its head. It swelled and split its sides, and all around it others did the same.

As the first flower opened, Wallop eyed it in bemused horror. It was as big as a milk pail, with four round, ivory petals that mirrored the moon. Nearby, a second and a third flower opened. More and more upturned their blank, creamy faces.

Wallop could stand no more – even for Freya's sake. With a violent snort, she bounded away from the house, kicking out at the flowers until drifts of huge, pale petals floated in the air.

She galloped off towards the cow shed, only to find more plants growing there. There were giant flowers around the hay barn, the hencoop, and all the farm buildings. The biggest of all sprouted from the dung heap. Wallop sought refuge in the middle of the Long Meadow with its familiar sorrel and buttercups. There she stood all night, twitching with unwelcome dreams.

21

Gardens

Rab woke abruptly, with a strong sensation of being watched. He blinked several times.

'Lilies in the pond,' he said aloud. 'I'm still dreaming. Aren't I?' It felt like morning, but the light that filtered through the ceiling was greener than normal. All around him stared pale flower faces, huge and round and blank as empty dinner plates.

Rab put out a cautious hand to stroke a flower. A petal came away at his touch, as thin as tissue and as smooth as butter, with a faint, silvery perfume. Rab watched it sway languidly to the floor, and kicked Gamaran on the ankle.

'Wake up! Something's happened.'

'Again?' groaned Gamaran. He opened his eyes and sat up with a start, gasping, 'The Night Flowers!'

'It certainly does,' said Silas, uncoiling a green tendril from his leg.

'Oh, my,' said Gamaran weakly. He thought,

When night flowers like white lamps bloom,
        And sadly light up every room...
I've forgotten the rest. But I wrote that two years ago.
What are they doing here, now?

He looked over at the witch, who was struggling with
a plant for control of her knitting. The stems had
grown through it as well as round it.

'Blinking things! This isn't what I meant at all!
There's been a mistake. Stop growing, will you? Purl
two, knit three, slip stitch over?' begged Tulip
desperately.

'You've got gardens,' said Swinula. 'Isn't that what
you asked for?' She was twisting a dozen green stems
into a wreath, which she placed on Porphyry's head. 'I
name you Queen of Pigs.'

'Those spells are stronger than I thought,' said Tulip,
worried. 'Now which did I use?' she mumbled to
herself. 'Was it the cat's paw knit or the lace rib stitch?
Just think, all those years, I never realised...'

'You certainly didn't use a cat,' said Rab. He lifted up
the leaves to peer beneath. 'All the animals have gone.
All those toads and rats, just disappeared. And I
thought they really liked me...'

Gamaran felt in his pocket. The quert nibbled gently
at his fingers. Could these really be the night flowers
from his poem? They were much bigger and tougher
than he'd imagined. Their strength was frightening.

They'd tilted the flagstones in the floor. Pushing up
between them, they grew waist high from the black
earth that spilt out beneath.

He stared up at the glass ceiling. Newly crazed with cracks, it dripped with dangling roots like festoons of dirty, tattered lace.

'Just look at that!' said Gamaran in awe. 'They're even growing through the glass!'

'What?' Rab jumped up and studied the ceiling. 'They've forced their way through the cracks. We might just have a chance of breaking through the ceiling now!'

'Not with my leg again,' warned Silas.

'I won't need it. Just a leg up.'

Gamaran obliged. Balancing on his shoulders, Rab pushed, grunting, at a shattered corner of the ceiling. With painful creaks and splinterings, it began to heave upwards.

'It's giving way!' cried Rab. 'It's breaking up! We can get out!'

'Even if we climb up there, we'll still be in the palace,' said Silas dampeningly.

'So what? We'll soon be out of it! Tulip, you're a genius! You've done it! Out of the dungeons at last! No more bread and water. I can't wait to sit down to a proper meal, and sleep in a proper bed!'

'A bed? I thought you had other plans,' said Swinula with a frown.

Rab failed to hear her. 'Come on, Gamaran!' he urged. 'Hoist me higher! It's working loose. We're free!'

22

Free

'Free!' echoed Gamaran in wonder. He felt a poem stirring in him, but merely murmured, *'Priceless*, 4 letters. How will we avoid being caught?'

'It's a jungle up there, from the look of it! All we'll have to do is skulk through the undergrowth.'

'Thanks to Tulip,' added Swinula, and gave the witch one of her unnerving smiles.

'Glad you appreciate it,' said Tulip stiffly. She wasn't thrilled at all, but rather anxious. The night flowers were not in the least what she'd expected. When she had cast her knitting pattern, she'd been thinking of posies of primulas and violets; nice tasteful little blossoms, not these snaky moon-faced monsters with the power to break apart the Palace. To tell the truth, she was becoming scared at the strength of her own magic.

Still, it would be nice to get home to Cranford and a cup of tea. 'I'll be glad to see my familiar again,' she said. 'Hope he hasn't been terrorising the neighbourhood!'

Quick as a knife the pig-girl answered. 'Oh, but you

won't be going home just yet, will you? Not until we've found the Sorcerer – you and Rab and me. You know, to force him to tell us what he's done with the Princess and wreak terrible revenge.'

'Oh! Yes. Though, actually,' said Rab, 'I just thought, perhaps I should go back to the farm first...' He faltered under her incredulous gaze. 'Only for a short time, of course. But I'm worried about my gran. I really should go back and mend the well.'

'What about that poor princess you were going to rescue?'

'I still am. I'm just thinking of my gran,' said Rab, who was also thinking of a hot bath and supper and his own bed. He felt sure heroic tasks were best tackled on a full stomach.

'Silas can go back to the farm for you!' said Swinula. 'He'll look after your gran.'

'No, that wouldn't be right.'

'Be a pleasure,' said Silas with a bow.

'You can't walk all the way to Withy Farm,' protested Rab. 'Not with a wooden leg! Anyway, you don't know where it is.'

'Withy Farm,' said Silas thoughtfully, 'away up east by the river? I can walk that far all right.'

'Then that's settled,' said Swinula. 'Rab? You're not *afraid*, are you? I may be only a pig-girl, but even I'm not scared of a stupid old sorcerer. I bet he's all bluff and bluster like my dad. What are you afraid of?'

'I'm not!' said Rab. 'I just meant that at some point—'

'Good. And Gamaran can join us.'

'What for?' Rab asked jealously. If he was going to be a hero, he didn't want to share the honours.

'He might come in handy. And of course we must have Tulip. Her magic is as powerful as any wizard's!'

My magic? thought the witch. I suppose it must be. Never knew I had it in me. But to pit myself against a sorcerer...What spell could I use against Tarcorax himself? I'll need a whole cardigan, at least.

She fiddled fretfully with her knitting, to give herself time to think.

'Your spells have all worked brilliantly so far!' added Swinula. 'We're relying on you, Tulip.'

'I know you are,' said Tulip grumpily. 'I wish you wouldn't. All right! I'll come.'

23

Seeds

A flower was opening beneath the Sorcerer's nose. He closed his eyes briefly as its shimmering scent reached him. It reminded him of his dead wife; of her favourite soap, of a bath full of silver bubbles. He pulled out a large black handkerchief and blew his nose. Pollen always made it run.

The night flowers had rooted themselves in his carpets, and three footmen were now busy hacking away at their stems. Throughout the castle the same chopping and uprooting was going on, although it seemed that for every plant cut down, another grew elsewhere.

One of his demons began to materialise.

'Got him?' demanded Tarcorax instantly.

'Well—'

'I told you to find him! Those were my orders!'

'But—'

'*Get* him. Otherwise I don't want to see you again! Do you understand?'

'But—'

'If you appear once more without the culprit,' snarled Tarcorax, 'you will be blown to smithereens!'

'That's not fair...' The demon's wail faded out, along with its body.

'Idiot,' grumbled Tarcorax. 'I'm surrounded by idiots. And this one's *clever*, whoever he is.'

He ran an impatient hand down the gryphon's cool neck. A tuft of glass fur snapped off at his touch.

'I've got a challenger, Hieronymus,' he said. 'I've got an enemy. There can be no doubt about it.'

'No one can challenge you,' whispered the gryphon, in a voice like the tinkling of glass.

'Can't they? I thought the poetry was just a fool's trick. But then the animals, and now these monstrous flowers...whoever's doing this is no fool. They're using my own Rules against me.'

The gryphon felt another clump of fur break off as the Sorcerer's fingers tightened. He didn't mind. He didn't mind the flowers either; they were an improvement on the bats and owls and moths that had besieged the tower in their hundreds the previous day.

'What next?' muttered his master. 'What's he got in store for me?'

Between the gryphon's feet, an ivory flower sighed softly. Its petals opened wider; curled right back, turned brown and withered before his eyes. They fell from the stem. A round black seed-head was left behind.

Even as Hieronymus bent his head to it, it burst with a faint pop, scattering small red seeds all over him. They tinkled musically as they rained upon his back and rattled to the floor.

'*Strong* magic,' murmured Tarcorax.

24

Out

Seeds showered in sudden, unexpected bursts all over Rab as he crouched in the undergrowth. Flower after flower was wilting and then seeding, in a series of gentle pops, just above his head. Luckily the leaves showed no sign of withering. The corridor was still waist-high in rustling greenery, concealing him as he waited for the others to climb out of the dungeon.

Tulip appeared, complaining, in the hole in the glass floor. Rab caught her wrists and hauled her up. She was followed by Silas, the pig, Gamaran, and lastly Swinula, who clambered agilely up a rope of twisted stems, then poked her head above the leaves to reconnoitre.

'Aha! Kitchens that way,' she said.

'How do you know?'

'Sausages,' said the pig-girl cryptically. 'From the kitchens you can get out to the kitchen garden, and over the orchard wall. Silas, that's the way you need to go.'

'Over a wall?' said Silas doubtfully. 'I can walk for ever, but I'm not too sure about walls. I'll need a hand with them.'

'I'll go with you,' said Gamaran reluctantly. He really wanted to stay and see what happened next, but how could an elderly one-legged ex-pirate manage walls on his own?

Swinula was put out. 'But we need you!'

'No, we don't. I shouldn't think he's much use in a fight,' said Rab, eyeing Gamaran's lanky, clumsy limbs.

'Well, I'd certainly appreciate the company,' said Silas, much relieved. 'Come on, then, Gamaran my lad! No use hanging about.' Standing up, he ploughed off noisily through the shrubbery.

'Well, off you go!' said Rab with faint contempt. 'We'll sort out the Sorcerer.'

'No, wait!' protested Swinula, but Gamaran had already set off after Silas, who was crunching down the corridor at a great rate.

At first, Gamaran ducked low in the undergrowth at every step, until he realised that there was nobody to hide from. After a few turns the plant-choked passage brought them to the kitchen.

'So this is where everyone is!' he breathed.

Inside the vast kitchen, a battalion of maids, cooks and footmen waged a tight-lipped battle against the night flowers. The stems snaked from the cupboards, the ovens, the sinks, the flour-bins, from every crack and cranny, and wherever they were ripped up, they began to sprout again from the remaining roots. There was a constant rattle of seeds hitting the floor.

A single soldier lounged against an oven, supervising. 'You've missed one over there!' he shouted, and helped himself to a piece of pie.

'Do as I do,' advised Silas. Calmly he began to copy the servants, tearing tendrils from a cupboard by the door, then from the shelves next to the cupboard. Slowly he worked his way around the kitchen. Gamaran followed him, diligently pulling up handfuls of vines and armfuls of leaves as he went.

Within a few minutes they reached the outer door. When the soldier turned aside to grab another slice of pie they slipped out unobserved, into the salad beds.

'That was easy!' said Gamaran, picking his way through the lettuce.

'Too easy,' said Silas doubtfully. 'Let's find the orchard. I wonder who else is usually on guard?'

They scuttled through fruit bushes and between apple trees that were almost smothered by the vines of the night flowers. They had nearly reached the wall when something brought them to an unexpected halt.

'Look down there,' said Gamaran, his voice hushed. 'Do you think...?'

Together they studied the mound of fresh earth beneath the apple tree.

'It's a bit short for a grave,' said Silas at last. 'And if Tarcorax *had* murdered his daughter, surely he wouldn't bury her in the kitchen garden?'

'Who's to say? I'd suppose we'd better look,' said Gamaran unwillingly. Dropping to his knees by the mound, he began to dig through the soft earth with his hands.

'I can feel something,' he said after a while. 'Feels like clothing. Just a minute...' He scrabbled in the soil, grimacing. 'Here we are... let me get the soil off... Oh, no. Oh, that's dreadful! That's *horrible*...'

Silas watched mutely as Gamaran brushed away the earth. It was a silk dress, pink as a prawn, festooned with pea-green ribbons, embellished with a whiskery filigree of crimson thread and sparkling with thousands of tiny purple sequins. Silas shook his head, speechless.

'It's... hideous,' he said at last.

'No wonder somebody buried it!'

'Yes. But who?'

Before Gamaran could answer, the air above him shimmered. Rippling like water, it abruptly fizzed into the shape of a grinning demon.

'Where are *you* going?' the demon demanded, twirling its tail.

'Oh, nowhere much,' said Silas vaguely.

'Too right!' sneered the demon. 'Down in the dungeons is where you – uh, oh.' Its expression grew worried; its body started to spark as if it was short-circuiting.

'What, I can't appear *anywhere*?' it wailed. 'But that's not *fair*! I don't like being smithereens!' And suddenly it exploded in a loud orange fireball. Gamaran thought he heard a last, faint disappearing echo: 'Not fair!' Then there was nothing left but the smell of sulphur, hanging in the air.

'Come on!' cried Gamaran. 'Before any more of them arrive!'

Letting the extraordinary dress fall back into its grave, he took a run at the wall, and swarmed up it using the stalks of the night flowers as a ladder. He scrambled to the top, then pulled Silas up after him. They half-climbed, half-fell down into the tangled mat of leaves on the other side.

Before them lay the town, newly and luxuriously wreathed in green. The sound of many axes came to their ears. Beyond the verdant town lay the golden fields and distant lilac hills. They were out.

25

Across

That morning, Freya couldn't get out of the house. The night flowers had barred the door. She had to slither painfully through a narrow window, fetch the axe and chop away the stems, while listening to Gran's insistent cries:

'But your porridge is ready now, Freya!'

As soon as Freya was out, she forgot all about porridge. She forgot the flowers. For overnight, the mist had grown.

It filled the valley like a huge, white, unflowing river. Its long arms reached out across the cow pastures. She could see Wallop and the other cows huddled at the end of the Long Meadow, as far away as possible from its embrace.

It was wash day. Normally Freya would take the laundry down to the riverside for a soak and scrub.

'I still can,' she told herself firmly. 'It's only river fog, that's all. There's nothing else down there. Nothing but the river. It's not as if I can get lost!'

All the same, she hesitated. The mist filled her with strange dread, but also with longing; as if once she entered that white cloud she might choose not to come out again. In the end, she turned her back resolutely on the looming bank of mist, and drew extra buckets of water from the well instead.

'I'll do the washing,' said Gran over breakfast. 'You see to the animals, since Holman's still poorly.'

Freya managed to unglue her teeth from the porridge.

'Holman's *gone*,' she said thickly, then shook her head at Saintly Gran's uncomprehending face, and went out to milk the cows. When she came back an hour later there were wet shirts all over the floor and a sock in the porridge pot; so she set out again to mend the walls. It was a slow, back-aching job, hefting stones up to fill the many gaps in the walls, and took her until well after noon.

Feeling as stooped and shrunken as a snail, Freya trudged home to the farmhouse. Someone was singing a sea shanty in the kitchen. A deep, growly, cheerful voice came ringing through the window; and then a little bald man stumped out of the house on a wooden leg, with a basket of washing.

'Hallo there and ahoy! Rab sent me,' he announced, 'to make sure that you were all right and hearty. I'm just giving your gran a hand with the laundry.'

'Rab?'

'We were in the dungeons together; just escaped this morning.' The little man stroked his beard apologetically. 'He's sorry he couldn't come himself, but there's some business he had to see to first.'

'Business?'

'Unfinished business with the Sorcerer. Don't worry, Rab's got a witch with him. He's a brave young man, your brother. Fire in his belly.'

Freya said nothing.

'I was like that once,' said the old man thoughtfully, and with a sigh turned back into the house. A moment later, a chorus of *Blow the Man Down* came breezing through the open window.

Freya hung the washing out on the line. It was not very clean. Someone else was watching her, from behind the big oak tree: a lanky boy with hair all on end, who didn't know what to do with his arms. He shambled towards her and awkwardly held out a small scrap of blue fluff in his hand. He said something that sounded rather like, 'Do you want a quert?'

But that made no sense. So Freya ignored him.

26

Up

Tulip Pennywort was not happy. She didn't like these endless glass stairs, for a start. Still less did she like the idea of where they might be leading.

'This place is an outsize, overgrown greenhouse,' she complained as she paused to puff on a landing. She would much rather be sitting at home with Cranford and a pot of tea, than battling through the jungle with two over-excited youngsters and a hungry pig.

On several occasions, their way had been barred by impenetrable thickets of night flowers. Creepers spiralled round every glass pillar, and looped across their path like crazy nets. When they couldn't wriggle through or climb over, they had to take a tortuous way around. Soon Tulip was completely lost.

And Rab was as jumpy as a flea. At every junction he stopped to argue with the pig-girl about which direction they should take. Usually, Swinula won. It was she who led the careful, convoluted way through the maze of weed-choked corridors and halls rattling with red seeds;

it was she who whisked them into hidden nooks whenever grumbling servants trudged past.

It was she who found the storeroom where they hid whilst a troop of guards next door had a leisurely lunch. They crept out at last to forage for the scraps of ham and cheese the guards had left behind.

And now, in the dim heart of the palace, it was Swinula who was urging them to climb the endless flights of stairs. The crystal staircases were cracking under the tight embrace of the night flowers, but that didn't seem to worry her as she clambered over the twining stems.

'Wait! Slow down!' Rab was panting. 'We must be twelve floors up by now!'

'No, only ten.' She stopped on a landing, where the leaves had grown into a concealing hedge.

'How many more?' gasped the witch. 'Well, I declare. Just look at that! The flowers have all gone, every one.'

It was true. The pale flowers had all seeded, and their petals withered away. Red pellets carpeted the floor, rolling under their feet as they walked.

Now the heart-shaped leaves were starting to curl up too, and blacken round the edges, so that Porphyry disdained to eat them. Something of the palace beneath could once again be seen. Shields and statues, plates and paintings glinted through the greenery.

'It's very grand up here,' said Rab disapprovingly. 'Why hang all these great big carpets on the walls? And I don't think much of those portraits. Snooty, aren't they?'

'Ancestors,' murmured the pig-girl.

'I like that suit of armour, though.' Rab knocked it on the breastplate with a hollow clung, and lifted the ornate sword from its gauntlet. This was more like a real sword! Better than his grandpa's old thing. It was long and light and keen, with a jewelled hilt. 'On guard!' He swiped the sword through the air with a flourish.

'Watch out!' grumbled Tulip, grabbing at her hat. 'You'll have someone's head off!'

'That's the idea!' Rab slashed again, drawing a figure of eight in the air. The sword hissed delightfully.

'*Magic* is our weapon,' said the pig-girl firmly. She raised an eyebrow at Tulip. 'Well?'

'Well, what?'

'Well, what are you going to do now?'

What indeed, thought Tulip, staring around the entangled palace. What can I do next, she wondered, after all those dratted plants? Tons and tons of vegetation. Millions of seeds. Extraordinary. I can hardly believe it was me.

'I'm just considering,' she announced with dignity.

Swinula picked up a handful of red seeds from the floor and let them fall through her fingers into a pattering pile.

'We've had poems,' she said reflectively. 'We've had pets. We've had gardens . . . Perhaps it's time for some toys.'

'Toys?' said Tulip blankly. 'Like tiddlywinks?'

'That wasn't quite what I had in mind.'

'Rag dollies? Tin soldiers?'

'Just see what you can do,' said Swinula.

'Now?' squealed the witch. 'Here?'

'Why not?'

Tulip racked her brains for a knitting pattern she hadn't tried yet. What about her nephew's birthday pullover? As a garment it had been a disaster, but it might make a decent spell.

'Purl one, twist left, knit four, repeat to last nine stitches,' she rehearsed under her breath. She glanced up the final flights of stairs that led to the Tower of Tarcorax. Fervently she wished she was at home, safely knitting her spell, instead of reciting it halfway up the Sorcerer's tower, with no idea of what the end result would be.

One thing was certain. Whatever it produced, it wouldn't be a baggy jumper with a tiny neck hole, and one sleeve upside down.

27

Porphyry

Porphyry, unlike the witch, was very happy indeed. For a start, she was full of tasty and nutritious greens, having gorged herself thoroughly all morning.

For another thing, she was an active pig with an enquiring mind. Her nose quivered expectantly and her sharp ears twitched as she trotted at Swinula's heels. This expedition was better by far than being penned in her sty, especially since she had the company of her beloved pig-girl. Her life had become considerably more interesting since Swinula had entered it.

Porphyry sniffed. The palace smelled of magic – a singed odour, like burning hair. It was full of the distant echoes of fascinating noises. Somewhere above her right now, there was a whole demons' chorus of fizzing and spitting, and a series of small, muffled bangs.

The pig-girl laughed, and Porphyry nuzzled her ankle contentedly. The old woman straightened up to glare at them before resuming her chanting and walking backwards in circles. Then, suddenly, she stiffened. Porphyry froze too, ears straining.

Hush, said the palace all around them. Sssshhh. It hissed like a wave dragging itself across a shingle beach. Porphyry almost expected to see the glass walls turn to water and pour away: but no, the sound was coming from the floor.

The carpet of small, red seeds began to move.

At first they just vibrated gently, as though someone had taken hold of the palace and was shaking it. Then they began to roll around of their own accord. They formed themselves into patterns: whorls, stars, spirals, drawn upon the floor in quick succession. The seeds tumbled together, and started to pile up on each other in steadily growing mounds.

Porphyry, not sure if she ought to be worried, nosed at her mistress.

'Toys,' crooned the pig-girl softly. 'Oh, we'll give you toys.'

Her hand stroked Porphyry's ear, and Porphyry shook her head as if an electric shock had run through her. But the pig-girl was smiling. Porphyry was happy. Life was good.

28

Toys

Hieronymus watched his master anxiously.

The last three demons had just been blown to smithereens, hissing and spluttering into orange fireballs, for daring to materialise empty-handed. That was all very well, but they wouldn't be so easy to recall, and who else was going to protect the palace? The guards were scattered all over the place, attacking the night flowers; Tarcorax was left with nobody to shield him except Hieronymus himself.

The gryphon's heart was heavy. Treading cautiously through the drifts of red seeds that threatened to send him skidding, he knew that he was worse than useless.

If only I was a dog, thought Hieronymus ruefully. A flesh-and-blood dog, that could leap upon an enemy without shattering, would be far more useful ... except, of course, that Tarcorax would never tolerate a common, hairy, smelly dog as his familiar. That was why Hieronymus had been created.

Something else was being created now, and not by

his master. The palace hummed and hissed. A shiver ran through it.

The red seeds shuddered and began to swirl. They rustled across the carpet, rolled themselves into a mound, and mushroomed into a quivering column, not unlike an ant hill, growing taller by the minute. Tarcorax and the gryphon gaped in puzzled, wary silence at this new, living statue, rust-red amidst the ranks of glass.

As they looked on, the column of seeds divided. Now it looked like a crude trunk on a pair of shapeless legs. Feet swelled out from the base. Arms budded from the top, and last of all, a head rose up.

The red shape wore a smile, but had no eyes. As unformed as a rough clay doll, it began to walk a little shakily towards the Sorcerer.

Tarcorax frowned at it. He raised his hand, snapped his fingers impatiently, and uttered a word of enchantment.

The red figure kept advancing. It sighed with every step.

Tarcorax took a pace backwards, pulling his cloak around him. He drew a hurried line on the floor with his staff, and began a more complex incantation.

The figure swayed. Ripples ran through it; it shed several of its fingers, which drummed onto the floor in a shower of red pellets. Then it steadied and began to walk on. Tarcorax took three more steps backwards, and found himself up against the wall.

Hieronymus was transfixed. If I were a faithful dog,

he thought, what would I do now? I must do what I can. I am, after all, bigger and harder than any dog.

With glass wings folded, he stalked into the path of the advancing figure. I am as hard as steel, he told himself, if somewhat more brittle. It tickles a little. No worse. As the figure touched him, he held his ground and pushed against it. He felt it disintegrating and heard the seeds rain down upon his back with a tuneful clatter.

And there's another one, thought Hieronymus, as a second shape reared up from the carpet. How peculiar; it's a rocking horse. All it needs is a push, and there it goes. And what's that one over there? It looks like a puppet.

The puppet was quite well-defined, as if whoever was moulding these figures was getting better at it. Shuffling up to Tarcorax, it raised a red arm and brought it down on the Sorcerer's head.

Tarcorax cried out as the arm shattered over him. Hieronymus barged into the puppet, and it collapsed.

'Come on,' said Tarcorax, breathing rather hard. 'Let's get out of here! More of them are growing already.'

Sure enough, each puddle of seeds was pulling itself together, flowing into a new mound. Tarcorax and the gryphon hurried past them before they could grow legs. Outside the Sorcerer's chamber, they slammed the doors tight shut.

Hieronymus blinked, unused to daylight. Here at the summit of the palace, blue sky poured in through the glass roof above. Dizzying flights of stairs zigzagged downwards through the black and withered trails of the night flowers.

Tarcorax, about to descend, stopped sharply. The staircase was lined on either side with rust-red statues. They stood as stiff and regular as oversized toy soldiers.

And between their red, unmoving ranks someone was climbing slowly up to meet him, holding an outstretched sword.

29

Swords

Rab gripped his sword hilt so firmly that his knuckles were white. This was to stop his hand shaking, rather than because of the weight of the sword. In fact, it now felt too light in his hand. He had a dreadful suspicion that it was meant only for decoration, and would bend or snap as soon as he tried to use it properly.

'Tell us where your daughter is!' he said. His voice came out higher than he would have liked.

The Sorcerer's face closed down. 'I have no daughter.'

'If you don't tell us where she is, I'll – I'll set cold steel to your flesh!'

'Oh, don't be ridiculous,' said the Sorcerer. 'Who are you? Ah, yes. I remember. I sent you to the dungeons.'

Rab leaped up two more steps, and found that the glass gryphon had placed himself in front of Tarcorax.

'Beware,' the gryphon whispered. 'Come no closer.'

'Yes, thank you,' said the Sorcerer rather sharply. 'I can still take care of myself! As *you*, young man, will discover if you don't get out of my way right *now*!'

Rab glanced quickly over his shoulder. Tulip and

Swinula were both out of sight, the cowards, skulking somewhere behind him round the bend in the stairs. He cursed them silently. It was far too late for him to retreat and join them now. He would have to keep going.

'Tell me where the princess is,' he said stubbornly. 'What did you do to her? Is she dead? Where is she? You can't come past until you tell me.'

The Sorcerer's eyes narrowed.

'Brave of you,' he commented, 'but not very wise.' He raised his hand and pointed a finger at Rab; and then his expression changed.

There was a sighing in Rab's ears. The ranks of red soldiers were gradually changing shape, until they were soldiers no more. Now they wore long, ribboned gowns, with red hair flowing down their shoulders, a coronet upon each identical red head.

'That's Amaranth!' breathed the Sorcerer. His eyes flashed. '*You're* not making these!' he said harshly. 'Who is it? Who's there with you?'

'It's me.' The voice of Tulip Pennywort rang out below. 'All right, all right, don't push me!'

She stepped into view. 'It's me, O Sorcerer, and I don't give a fiddle for your glass gryphon and your dinky little demons and your precious rules and regulations.' She wagged a bony finger at him as she got into her stride. 'It's all just playing at being king, that's what it is! It's high time you grew up and faced your responsibilities. Took some notice of other people. But dear me, oh no. You're far too important to do that. Hoity-toity!'

The Sorcerer stared down at her with incredulity in his

face. Rab winced with embarrassment at the witch's crooked hat and the rolled-up knitting poking out of her pocket. All the same, he couldn't help being impressed by her vigour.

'Oh, you're very high and mighty, way up here in your palace, playing with your spells!' she cried, as she plodded up the stairs. 'Then just because you have a dust-up with your daughter, you have to throw a tantrum and take it out on everybody! What kind of way is that to run a country? Nothing but bad temper! Well, I'm going to teach you a lesson you won't forget.'

The Sorcerer found his voice at last. '*You?*' he mocked. 'A wart-charmer? An amateur wand-waver?'

'Just look around you!' responded the witch tartly. 'Like what you see? You ain't seen nothing yet!'

'She means it!' blurted Rab. 'This is your last chance. Repeal your laws. Set free your daughter. Otherwise, you'll see such magic as you've never dreamed of in your life!'

Tarcorax looked hard at him again, all trace of laughter gone.

'You cannot defeat me,' he said. 'Don't try!'

'We have to try!'

'How do you like our toys?' cackled the witch below. 'Pretty, ain't they?'

There was a hissing like a thousand serpents all along the stairs. Rab nearly fell down them in alarm.

The two long rows of princesses still stood on either side; but on each head, the flowing hair had turned to a tangle of red snakes that hissed and writhed; and each right hand now held a crimson sword.

110

30

Shepherd

Gamaran sat on a hillside pretending to guard Freya's sheep, while actually watching her roof.

Luckily the sheep weren't doing much, apart from eating, and baa-ing surprisingly loudly. If one of them fell over a cliff or started having a lamb, he supposed he would have to do something, but he had no idea what.

He'd spent all afternoon trailing around after Freya, asking, 'Can I help?' at frequent intervals. Mostly she seemed not to hear. Sometimes she gave him things to carry, although it was quickly evident to Gamaran that she herself could do everything (including carrying things) both faster and better than he could.

She could chop wood with a speed and skill that made him cringe; he couldn't chop an onion without hacking his finger. She ordered cows around with absent-minded ease, and they obeyed. They didn't even try to kick her.

Just look at her now, thought Gamaran, up on that

roof, mending the thatch. She knows how to *thatch*! I'd just slide off in an avalanche of straw. And when the red seeds started making things, she simply whacked them to bits with a spade, and let the hens loose on them to eat them up. She's extraordinary. There she sits, making a roof, and the sky revolves around her. I wish I could do something to impress her. I wish I was more useful.

At least he was good at crosswords. Maybe Freya would like a crossword.

Gamaran pulled a crumpled piece of paper from his pocket, drew a twelve by twelve grid, and carefully wrote *spade*, *straw*, *plough* and *turnip* in it. He frowned long at the paper, but could think of no other words to fit.

'Ploughed over,' he murmured, gazing back at the roof. 'I'm being ploughed over, turned upside down and inside out. A crossword's not enough.'

Ten minutes later, he turned the paper over and began to think of words that would rhyme with Freya.

31

Silas

Silas sat darning the socks by the stove. Opposite him, Saintly Gran was smiling and nodding as she rocked her chair.

'The sea takes hold of you,' explained Silas. 'I never meant to stay at sea. I always meant to come home again, but the sea wouldn't let me. I had to return to it, even after that shark took my leg and piracy was the only way back. The sea still called me. The endless song of the sea – it never stops, it never fails ... Even at dead of night there's always the friendly slap and clap of the waves against the ship. It's like a giant set of arms holding you in your cradle, and you being rocked to and fro.'

Gran rocked her chair and nodded.

'It takes care of you, the sea, one way or another,' went on Silas. 'Not that it's all easy. The sea spray, now: it's as if it never stopped raining! I was never dry, my whole time at sea. Twelve years of damp! But it keeps you on your toes.'

'Oh, yes indeed,' said Gran.

'You'd like the smell of the sea,' Silas told her, 'so sharp and new. Every day fresh, no cares, no worries. No house or farm or family to drag you down. And there's always movement. Beats a rocking chair hollow! I'll take you on a boat one day, and you can feel for yourself.'

Gran smiled, and Silas hummed happily. Since no demons appeared to drag him back to the dungeons, he hummed a little louder, and then burst into full-throated song.

There was a startled cry above his head, a faint slithering noise, and a loud thump just outside the window.

Silas threw open the window and peered out.

'Next time, *warn* me when you're going to make that noise,' said Freya, sitting in a heap of straw. She picked herself up painfully and hobbled back towards the ladder.

Gamaran was galloping down the far hillside, waving frantically. As Silas watched, he tripped over a sheep. Silas waved back, and closed the window.

'I'll make that a promise,' he said to Gran. 'It's not been an easy life for you, cooped up in here. Sheep and turnips and porridge, year in, year out. No life for a lady, I can see that now. So when Rab comes back, off to sea we'll go together. How'd you like to learn to dance the hornpipe?'

32

Sunset

Freya's fingers busied themselves once again with the thatch. Her hands were hot, raw and itchy from handling the straw, so she ignored them, as if they were no part of her. Her mind was elsewhere. She raised her eyes from the roof to seek out the distant glitter of the Glass Palace, glowing against the evening sun.

'Come back, Rab,' she said to the sunset. 'Stop being such a hero, please. I don't want a hero for a brother. Especially not a dead one.'

She glanced over at the sheep-speckled slopes, where Gamaran was being chased uphill by an irritated ram. 'Those pirates you sent aren't much use. I can't do it all by myself any more. I'm so tired of being alone. Come back, Rab, *please*.'

She knew she was talking to nobody. The late heat of the sun pressed down upon her and made the straw itchier than ever.

Yet despite the sun's warmth, down in the river valley mist was forming again already – too soon, far too soon. Although Freya tried not to look that way, she could smell its odour: like damp earth, like the bottom of the well. This was not right. It ought not to be there. Not now.

The night flowers had disturbed her, a little. The red seed figures that followed had worried her a little more, not least in case they poisoned the hens. But *this* – this was something else again. The sun had not even set.

Could this be the work of Rab's witch too? She was powerful enough, that was certain. The night flowers had clothed every building Freya could see from the farm to the palace, trussing them overnight in thick green nets.

But the mist was different. The mist came only *here*. Only to this portion of river that looped round Withy Farm, and nowhere else. All morning it had lingered, until the midday sun had driven it back, shrinking it to a wispy veil above the water. And then the footprints had been clear to see.

Freya felt a tightening in her throat which neither the pets, nor the flowers had made her feel. The mist shadowed her mind like a dreadful memory that would not let itself be forgotten. It pulled at her. Why had it come?

She spoke aloud again, this time to the Dawn Walker, who would not hear because he could not exist.

'There's no one sick,' she said urgently. 'There's no one dying, no one for you, no reason to stay. Go away, please.'

Away to the west, beyond the palace, the clouds drew long, red, ragged stripes against the sky. Through their midst, slowly, gracefully, a black plume began to rise above the palace towers. A feather of smoke, growing, widening, opening into a whole peacock's tail.

The Glass Palace was on fire.

33

Smoke

Tulip's day was getting worse by the minute.

She stood at the top of the stairs and mopped her brow with her knitting. Her hand was shaking. This time, she'd truly terrified herself.

She'd barely even begun her latest spell (triple basket stitch) when it seemed that the world tilted. The palace creaked beneath her, as if in a high wind. The smell of scorched hair became stronger than ever.

The Sorcerer's eyebrows shot up. He exclaimed under his breath, rapidly unbarred his doors again and whisked himself and the glass gryphon back inside his tower.

Rab waved the sword triumphantly. 'Yes! We've got him on the run!'

'Can't you *feel* it?' hissed the witch. 'Can't you *smell* it?' Magic buzzed in her ears and made her skin tingle; it drew sparks from the pig-girl's hair as she climbed the staircase to join them.

The red statues were rapidly melting down. They

dissolved back into seeds which cascaded away down the stairs. They were no longer needed, thought Tulip apprehensively. Something much, much bigger was on its way.

Through the scorched smell there came a darker, sourer stink. Tulip recognised it: blood. Her hair stood on end. A shadow fell upon her through the glass above, and she dared not look up. She wished hopelessly that it might just be a storm cloud, but she knew that it was not.

Swinula drew a long breath. When she stretched a hand out to caress the rigid, wide-eyed pig, miniature needles of lightning juddered from her fingers.

'Look up,' she said. Her face was flushed, elated.

Tulip looked down, wishing herself back in the dungeons, anywhere deep and hidden, anywhere but here. She heard Rab gasp in disbelief.

'Scales!' he whispered. 'The sky is full of scales!'

Swinula grinned exultantly. 'Look, Porphyry!' she said. 'See what no other pig has seen, and lived. We've done something that all the Sorcerer's magic cannot equal. We've brought him *stories*! We've brought him the dragon!'

34

Down

'This is *not* the work of that old witch,' said Tarcorax. 'She couldn't turn a tadpole into a toad. There are things going on—'

The crystal chandelier fell from the ceiling with a crash, demolishing a glass leopard. The ceiling itself appeared oddly blurred. As Tarcorax blinked, it began to sag and drip. The glass was melting.

All over it, stalactites of molten glass were forming. Shiny droplets gathered on their tips, and fell, pinging off the glass animals, becoming flat, transparent pebbles as soon as they hit the floor.

'Fire and brimstone!' cursed Tarcorax. 'My chandelier! Come on, Hieronymus, before the whole roof falls in. Don't look at me like that! How can I fight if I don't even know who I'm fighting? If those idiotic imps had done their job—'

A large drop of glass fell on Hieronymus, chipping his shoulder.

'This way,' said Tarcorax. Kicking a rug from the floor,

he lifted the trap door concealed beneath and urged Hieronymus down the narrow spiral staircase below.

Preparing to descend behind the gryphon, he paused before he let the trap door close. A rotten, smoky reek seeped through the room. On every wall the tapestries were smouldering. The portrait of his missing daughter burst into sudden flame.

Tarcorax raised his staff. For form's sake more than anything, he shouted:

'*O flammae extenuamini! O fla—*'

The ceiling fell in with a resounding smash. The bandaged throne exploded, for a second time. Tarcorax caught a momentary glimpse of a huge belly covered in brown scales; and then the trap door slammed, shutting it out.

'Dragon,' he told the gryphon matter-of-factly as they clambered down the narrow stairs. 'Only a dragon.'

The spiral staircase came out, many dizzying circles later, inside a broom cupboard in a little used and particularly grimy section of the palace.

'Can't see a thing,' complained the Sorcerer, sweeping aside cobwebby brushes with a careless clatter.

There was a louder, thunderous crash far above him. It sounded as if the whole tower had collapsed.

'I can only hope,' said Tarcorax as they hurried along a dingy passage, 'that whoever is responsible has brought the roof down on top of themselves. Serve them right for meddling with dragons!' For Hieronymus's sake, he spoke scornfully, as if he knew all about dragons and their causes.

In fact, he was aware that he did not know nearly enough. The only dragons that Tarcorax had met had been small and immature, not much more than twenty candle-power. He had never conjured up a full-blown dragon, and was not at all sure that he could if he tried.

'It's not as simple as calling up a demon,' he said aloud. 'Demons are biddable. They have no backbone. Bending a dragon to your will is a different matter altogether.'

'It takes a strong will?' whispered the gryphon.

'It does indeed. That witch—' He halted at the sound of another distant crash.

'And then, *holding* a dragon is something else again,' he finished grimly.

35

Dragon

Swinula's smile had gone. She was pale and sweating.

Rab was pleased to see this. She'd been too smug for his liking all along, acting as if nothing could frighten her or her pig. She'd been too bossy by half as well; but who had climbed the stairs to face the Sorcerer? Not she. So he was glad it was her turn to be frightened for a change.

'Stop worrying,' he told her curtly. 'We're safe enough here.'

When the roof had begun to drip, they had taken flight back down the long stairs in panic. Rab had to catch Tulip several times as she stumbled.

Once they had made the long, frantic descent, however, it had been easy to get out of the palace. They simply had to step through a huge hole melted in the wall. Any guards they met had been too busy running away to challenge them.

Out in the gardens, they halted, crouching in the shelter of an avenue of elm trees, to watch the dragon wreak its havoc on the palace. Now that he was safe, Rab felt no fear, just a pure thrill of excitement. *This* was really showing the Sorcerer! This proved they meant business! This would teach Tarcorax a lesson!

For the dragon was immense. It laboured upwards with slow, noisy beats of its leathery wings, then hovered against the evening sun. It did not gleam: it was as dull, brown and ugly as an old boot. Even the glow of inner heat that reddened its skin did nothing to make it beautiful.

It hung in the air, blotting out the sun, and then it dived. Down it plunged on the palace, belching fireballs over the remaining rooftops. Wherever it breathed, the glass blushed and smouldered. Beneath the smoke, the Tower of Tarcorax had already disintegrated; and now the four guard towers began to bulge and sag, and weep glass tears.

'Like a jelly left out in the sun,' said Rab admiringly, and he tapped Tulip on the shoulder. 'Well done! Just what we needed.' Tulip did not answer. She was chewing a corner of her sleeve, and whimpering.

The dragon beat its heavy wings and rose aloft again, above the cloud of black smoke that now enveloped the palace. It cast its huge and hideous head around, as if seeking for something else worthy of attention.

The head turned towards Rab. He caught its deep red eye, and dropped his gaze in a hurry.

The dragon banked round, then swooped towards them, its wings whumping. Rab dived to the ground. The pig, squealing, tried to burrow underneath him.

Rab felt a hot gale rush across his back. There was the sharp crack of splitting wood close by. The wing beats throbbed loudly overhead, and then passed on.

Warily, Rab raised his head. The tree above him was split from top to base, its branches charcoal. The grey leaves crumbled to a fine ash and were blown away in the breeze.

Towards the east, a black shadow grew smaller against the darkening sky. The dragon was departing. Rab sat up. There was a strong, rank smell of wood-smoke, rotten meat and burning hair.

'That was amazing!' he told Tulip, who sat shivering beside him. 'Wonderful! The best yet. I can't think how you're going to beat that!'

Tulip just croaked in reply.

Swinula was standing, white-faced, with her arms wrapped tightly round a tree. Her eyes were closed; her lips moved silently.

'Don't worry!' Rab said pityingly. He would never have expected her to crack up like this. 'It's all right. It's gone now.'

'It's not supposed to *go*,' said the pig-girl hoarsely. 'I didn't tell it to *go*.'

'What?'

'It's supposed to stay, and obey. I can't hold it. It's too strong.'

She slumped against the tree, pressing her forehead on the bark. It's too much for her, decided Rab, her mind is giving way.

'Never mind!' he reassured her. 'The nasty dragon's

125

all gone now. I'll tell Tulip to do something a bit smaller next time.'

'Tulip?' The pig-girl's eyes slowly focused on the shivering witch. 'I wish she could.'

'Look,' said Rab, exasperated, 'just pull yourself together, will you? It's only a bit of magic!'

Swinula's eyes snapped fully open. 'A bit of magic? A *bit*? I summon the biggest dragon this land has seen in five hundred years, and you call it a *bit of magic*?'

Rab's head began to whirl. 'But you – but she—'

'Don't be so brainless! Tulip couldn't conjure up a woodlouse. Of course it was me, all along!'

'But – how—'

Swinula bent down to the witch. 'Can you remember any holding spells?' she asked urgently.

Tulip shook her head feebly. 'Was none of it me, then?' she croaked.

'None at all. You were just camouflage.'

'Well, thank the stars above for that! It had me quite worried.' The witch sat up straighter and adjusted her hat. 'It's gone east,' she said, sounding more like herself. 'Towards the hills. Did you tell it to go east?'

'No.'

'That'll surprise a few people.'

'It'll do more than that,' said Swinula grimly. 'It'll ravage the fields. Burn down the farmsteads. Kill all the livestock just for the joy of it.'

'Let's hope that's all it kills,' said the witch, her voice doom-laden. Rab felt a chill finger stroke down his spine.

126

'Hang on,' he said. 'East? Farmsteads? My home's that way!'

Tulip shook her head. 'Too bad, dearie.'

'But you've got to stop it!'

'I can't,' said Swinula in despair. 'I don't know how. I never learned magic properly, I was finding out as I went along.'

'Playing at it,' said Tulip caustically.

'I'm *good* at it!' fired Swinula. 'You've got to be good, to call up a dragon – especially one that size! Only now I can't control it.'

'Then who can?' asked Rab numbly.

'No one. No one can. Except, possibly—'

36

Amaranth

'My father,' murmured Swinula.

Tarcorax was stalking over the scorched grass towards them, quivering with anger.

'Just look at my palace!' he roared at the witch, gesturing at the smoking, molten, shapeless ruin behind him. '*Look* at it!'

Hieronymus stepped over to the pig-girl and knelt carefully at her feet. Tarcorax, puzzled, frowned at his gryphon and stared at the pig-girl; first with wrath, then with enquiry, and finally with wonder.

'Amaranth?' he said hoarsely. 'Amaranth! My daughter! My lost daughter!' He stretched out his hands to her. 'Where have you *been*? You don't know what you've done to me! Where have you been hiding? Why did you bury your beautiful dress? Just look at you now! What on earth are you wearing? – And why have you dyed your lovely hair? It's the colour of soot! Have you been rolling in the mud? Amaranth, you're filthy!'

'That's the dirt of your dungeons,' said Amaranth sternly.

'My dungeons!' Tarcorax looked shocked.

'You should try them yourself.'

'But the dungeons are for the common people, not for the likes of you, even if you do look like a beggar! . . . and in the name of all the stars, Amaranth, why is that pig following you around?'

'It's a fine pig,' said Amaranth chillingly. 'At least it's *real.*' Hieronymus rose to his feet and turned away.

'Fine people with you, too, no doubt!' exploded Tarcorax. 'What sort of company is this for you to keep? Why are you mixing with hags and guttersnipes? You are a princess, and should behave like one!'

'She does,' said Tulip. 'Believe me. All the time.'

But a new understanding was dawning in the Sorcerer's eyes.

'The magic!' he breathed. 'The animals, the poetry! It wasn't this old witch at all, was it? It was you! I *knew* those spells were strong! You see, you can do magic! I *knew* you had it in you! And without tuition, too. Amazing! The seeds almost had me worried! And the flowers were quite – quite remarkable.'

'I borrowed those,' said Amaranth sullenly. 'From one of the other prisoners. He had a head full of magic, he just didn't know it. The flowers weren't my idea.'

'But the power to make them grow was yours! You see what you could do with a little guidance?'

'Guidance?' said Amaranth.

'If only you'd come and asked me for advice, before calling up a dragon that destroyed half my palace—'

'We've got to stop that dragon!' burst out Rab. 'It's gone east, towards the hills!'

'Yes, I saw it leave. Good riddance.'

'But my home's that way!' said Rab desperately. He no longer cared for half a kingdom, or a princess for a bride – especially this princess. All he wanted was the safety of his farm and family.

'Well, what am I supposed to do about it?' demanded Tarcorax with irritation. 'Look at my palace! It's destroyed, melted down to its foundations! The work of thousands and the pride of generations – ruined! You can hardly expect me to weep over your wretched little hovel.'

'Oh, yes he can!' retorted Tulip. Marching up to the Sorcerer, she stood nose to nose with him so that he recoiled. 'That's exactly what we *do* expect of our ruler – not a bundle of useless laws made up in a fit of the sulks! And your show-off of a daughter's just as bad. *She* started this dragon. *You'd* better put an end to it! That's your job!'

'I'm not a knight,' the Sorcerer answered curtly. 'If it's out of my sight and out of my way, it can do what it likes. Now, if Amaranth had only had the sense to learn the proper spells and safeguards—'

'I can't control it!' shouted Amaranth. 'And it's heading over *your* town, through *your* kingdom, and is about to wreak terrible havoc all over *your* people!'

'*My* people,' said Rab, stricken. He recognised the

130

taut expression on the Sorcerer's face. 'You're afraid,' he said incredulously.

'Don't be absurd!' snapped Tarcorax.

'You can't control it either. Can you?'

'Of course I can! Am I Lord High Sorcerer for nothing?'

'Evidently,' said Tulip, staring at him with eyes like gimlets. Tarcorax reddened.

'I'll show you who's in command here!' Whirling round, he snapped at the gryphon. 'Carpet! Carpet, Hieronymus! Where's my flying carpet?'

'Burnt to ashes in the fire,' whispered the gryphon, its ears and tail drooping.

'Oh, excellent!' Tarcorax ran fevered fingers through his hair, then jabbed them at the witch.

'You! Broomstick?'

'Certainly not! I use my legs, young man, and so should you.'

'That'll take too long,' decided Tarcorax. 'It's getting dark already, and we'll never catch the dragon up on foot. If there's no carpet, we'll just have to think of something else...'

37

Visitors

Night came early to Withy Farm.

The remains of the sunset were shrouded in dark, billowing smoke that mushroomed from the distant palace. Out of the smoke came a flying speck, at first no bigger than a gnat. Then, coming closer, it grew into a bat, then a crow, then an eagle; then something bigger than all of these, bigger than anything that ever flew, except a dragon.

The cows bellowed in fear, and thudded in all directions. The panicky sheep skittered together across the hillside in wide, useless circles.

As the dragon swooped upon his flock Gamaran decided that it was time to end his short career as a shepherd. Vaulting the wall, he slid and tumbled down the hill, and collided with a large, excited cow.

'Dragon!' he shouted. 'It's a dragon! *Dragon!* Everybody hide!'

'Yes, I can see it,' said Freya. 'Calm down, Wallop. I won't let it get you. It's caught a sheep now; that'll keep it happy for a bit.' She began to pat the agitated cow.

'But aren't you bothered?' demanded Gamaran.

'Oh yes. But not about the dragon.'

'What do you mean? What else is there?'

'Look.' Freya pointed down into the valley. Full to the brim, it overflowed with pale mist.

'That fog?' said Gamaran blankly. 'But I'm talking about a dragon. We need to hide!' The blood ran quicker in his veins; never mind the dragon, Freya was actually *talking* to him. Well, partly to him, anyway. More to herself.

'It's always there, these days,' she said.

'It's only river fog,' said Gamaran. He had managed to ignore it until now, assuming that its oddness was part of the general oddness of things in the countryside.

'It's higher every day.' Freya evidently took this seriously.

'Damp grass?' suggested Gamaran vaguely.

'Someone walks in there at night,' said Freya.

Gamaran's blood seemed to slow again and thicken. 'The Dawn Walker,' he murmured. Then, wanting to reassure Freya, he went on, 'But he doesn't really exist. He's only an old story.'

'Yes. Just like dragons. Come on, Wallop, into the barn with you.' She threw her arm across the cow, and leaned on her shoulder as she led her away.

Gamaran blundered into the farmhouse. 'Fog!' he cried. 'I mean dragon!'

Silas was as unnaturally calm as Freya. 'Don't worry,'

he said. Gran's rocking chair clunked steadily on the flagstones.

'Don't *worry*? I said there's a dragon! It's sitting on a hilltop half a mile away tearing a sheep to bits!'

'Then it's busy, and won't hurt us,' said Silas reasonably. 'Now don't get Gran upset. It's Rab's dragon. It's Tulip's dragon. They'll sort it out. It'll fade just like the flowers did.' He lit the lamp, while Gran rocked in her chair.

'I wouldn't bank on that,' said Gamaran. His anxious gaze followed the flickering lamplight around the farmhouse...There was too much wood everywhere. And the thatched roof would burn off in minutes...

'We've got to get Gran out,' he cried. 'We've got to move her. Gran!' He shouted in her ear. 'You've got to move!'

'I'm too old to move,' said Gran firmly. 'Here I stay, until Rab comes home.'

'Wonderful woman,' said Silas. 'Steady as a rock. Not a shred of fear! Me, now, I've always been a bit of a coward. I remember the first time I went to sea—'

'Gran!' bellowed Gamaran, tugging at her arms. 'You've got to move! We'll all be frazzled!' Outside, he could hear an ominous noise; a rushing wind, a whirr in the air, faint, but growing louder. 'It's coming back! Help me, Silas. There must be somewhere we can hide her! Get her outside, down to the river! You can hide down in the valley, in the fog!'

But Silas's face turned grey. 'No,' he said. 'Not there.'

'Here I sit, and here I stay,' Gran declared.

The sound rose to a whining roar. Something very big and very fast whooshed right overhead.

'Freya!' wailed Gamaran. He dashed outside, and Silas hobbled after him.

Gran was left alone. Her mouth began to tremble.

'So you want to be rid of me,' she said. 'I never thought it would happen. Rab would never have cast me out this way.'

She wiped her eye with a trembling hand. 'You've already brought the wagon, have you? I know, you see. I can't hear it, but I feel its rumble. I *can* still feel. All right, then, I'll go. I'll move out. I expect you'll find things easier without me. But I won't complain.'

Hauling herself out of the rocking chair, she began to grope unsteadily towards the door.

38

Night

A full moon was rising, but the travellers did not need it to light their way. A hundred fires, small and large, were burning down below in the darkness, in a line all the way from the palace to the eastern hills. Tiny figures ran to and fro, beating at the flames; but too late for the cornfields and hayricks already blackened and smoking.

Rab lay on his stomach on the grass, clutching his sword for courage, and watching the fires flash past beneath him. They were like golden eyes in the darkness. A cold wind blew through his hair and clothes, making him shiver.

This was a terrible way to travel. Even a carpet would have been better, he decided. It wouldn't have been so damp, for a start, nor so perilously crumbly as a ten-foot slab of flying turf.

Tarcorax had sliced it from the palace lawns with the point of his staff. At a shout from the Sorcerer, it had torn itself from the earth and hovered, undulating, in the air. Now, as it flew along, the edge kept shedding lumps of soil and startled worms.

It was none too soon for Rab when the turf banked over Withy Farm and came in to land. He frowned at the farmhouse roof, which looked newly thatched – only that was impossible. It must be a trick of the moonlight.

With a rib-cracking thump, they landed in the field by the big oak tree. Rab, thoroughly winded, rolled slowly off the close-shaved lawn of the carpet and lay, wheezing, in the long fragrant grass of his own land. The pig galloped past him, followed by the others. Last of all limped Hieronymus, who had cracked one leg on landing.

'I thought you were the dragon!' cried a relieved Gamaran, running over to meet them. 'Rab! Tulip! Oh – Your Lordship! I didn't know it was you – I'm so sorry – beg your pardon—'

'All right,' said Tarcorax shortly. 'Pardoned. You're all pardoned. For the moment, not for ever. Now then, where's the dragon?'

'It was on that hill a while ago,' said Gamaran uncertainly. The dragon was nowhere to be seen. 'Perhaps it's gone behind it.'

'Or it might be down in that valley,' suggested Tulip.

The Sorcerer turned to scan his surroundings. He saw the lake of mist, shining palely in the moonlight, and became very still.

'Amaranth,' he said quietly. 'What else have you called up?'

'I don't know.' She shook her head wearily. 'I don't even know if I did that. But I can feel it too.'

'But what on earth possessed you—'

'I don't know! You *made* me do it! I just conjured up everything I could, because you made me so angry!'

'*I* made *you* angry? *I* was being perfectly reasonable! It was *you* who was being stubborn and childish.'

'Oh, you call all your stupid Rules perfectly reasonable, do you? You call throwing people into the dungeons for singing perfectly reasonable?'

Amaranth and her father scowled at each other.

'Excuse me,' said Freya. 'But can you please cure an old woman who's blind and deaf?'

'Of course not,' said Tarcorax curtly. 'I can't work miracles.'

'What a surprise! You always told me magic could do anything,' mocked Amaranth.

'DON'T LAUGH AT ME!' roared her father.

A body threw itself onto Rab's shoulder and clung there. It was Saintly Gran. 'Don't let them throw me out, Rab! You'll never make me move out, will you?'

'Move, Gran? Of course not! Gamaran, Silas, what's going on?' Rab demanded, brandishing his sword. 'Have you been threatening my gran? I should have known better than to trust a pirate!'

'If I had my cutlass in my hand, you wouldn't speak to me like that!' declared Silas.

'Find yourself a weapon, then, and I'll say it again!' cried Rab, waving his sword dramatically. Now that he'd recovered from his ride, and the dragon seemed to have disappeared, he was feeling much more heroic. He was back on his own ground and ready to fight for his family. 'Come on, then, Silas! Don't you run away, Gamaran! I'll teach you to upset my gran!'

Unfairness hides in juice tins, 9 letters,* thought Gamaran, flinching away. I wish I had a sword too. Why, the sun's rising. No, of course it isn't. Wrong time, wrong place... and that's not the sun, it's much too big... oh dear.

For over the top of the hill, incandescent in the darkness, lit by a furnace from within, rose the dragon, and its strident, pitiless cry drove the argument from every mouth.

---

* Answer: injustice (anagram of 'juice tins')

139

39

Fight

So the fight began.

Gamaran was rigid with excitement. This was the stuff of epic poetry. It was the sight of a lifetime: a combat straight out of ancient tales was about to be enacted before his eyes! He couldn't believe his luck.

As the dragon dived from the sky, his mind ran frantically through lists of words, trying to find the best description. It was so *big*, so *powerful*...

Enormous, massive, strapping, hefty, he thought. A mighty thunderbolt of stone! No, a monster sleek as polished leather, setting fire to all the heather...it's only grass, but that doesn't matter...Oh, those teeth! Like daggers! Like pinnacles! His mouth with spiny pinnacles he gnashes and his frightful whippy tail he lashes. I wish I had my notebook.

At the dragon's appearance Rab had shrunk away, retreating to his gran's side to put a protective arm around her shoulder. Gamaran could almost have thought Rab was hiding behind her, had he not known of Rab's daring.

It was Tarcorax who stepped forward to meet the dragon. To Gamaran's delight, four of the Sorcerer's demons appeared, looking a little fuzzy around the edges, and armed with long, snaky ropes. But when they tried to pinion the dragon's wings, they were shaken away as easily as drops of rain from an umbrella.

Or sparks from a bonfire, thought Gamaran excitedly. The demons fizzled out, and Tarcorax staggered backwards, letting his staff fall to the ground.

He looked dazed and shaken. But his daughter ran forward to seize his staff and take his place. Sparks leaped from her hair and crackled from her fingertips.

Gamaran gasped. At Amaranth's command, the great oak tree that stood in the field began to lean over the dragon, creaking as it twisted its branches round it, until the dragon was locked in its gnarled embrace. He thought, Oh, yes! With twiggy arms of steel the worm to strangle – oh. What rhymes with uproot?

The great tree was flung to one side as casually as a weed, and the dragon advanced. Its innards glowed red like the embers deep in a fire.

With white fire Amaranth answered it. Clouds gathered overhead, blotting out the moon, and spears of lightning stabbed downwards again and again. Thunder crashed and hammered at Gamaran's ears until he felt deaf and dizzy. But while the thunderbolts could hold the dragon back, they could not penetrate its armour.

The night wore on: the battle continued. When Amaranth faltered, Tarcorax rejoined her, the pair of them chanting spells in turn while Tulip shouted encouragement from the sidelines.

'Try the bone-blaster!' she would yell. 'Try the hawk-hammer! That's the stuff!' But she uttered no spells herself.

As for Rab, he still hung back with Gran and Silas by the farmhouse. Every so often he clutched his sword more tightly, muttering; but he did not interfere.

Gamaran was enraptured. This was an epic indeed! The field was burnt black. The fallen oak lay charred and leafless. Tarcorax's cloak hung in scorched ribbons from his shoulders. Time after time the dragon attacked, and time after time it was turned aside, clawing the air and spouting angry flame.

But Tarcorax and his daughter began to droop and stumble. At last they leaned upon each other in their exhaustion, and clasped each other tight.

Gamaran was moved. It was just what his heroic poem wanted: a human touch.

'These two at last in battle reconciled, the Sorcerer majestic and his child,' he recited. The pair of them fell to their knees, and did not get up.

Then, with an ugly jolt, Gamaran realised that they were probably going to lose.

And that he and everybody else was probably going to die.

His poem flew out of his head. 'Freya!' he cried. 'Where's Freya?' He bolted to the farmhouse.

Freya was not there. She was not with the little group huddled fearfully outside the house. She wasn't inside either; the thatch was blazing fiercely now from stray sparks, and the house was filling up with smoke. She wasn't in the barn, nor to be seen anywhere by either the cold moonlight or by the terrible fiery blaze of the dragon.

There was only one place Gamaran had not searched. Along the river, the bank of mist rose higher than ever before. It flooded out across the fields, a sinuous white wall.

Gamaran stopped short in front of it. He held out one hand, tentatively, and felt a chill run through his fingers. It was a wall of absolute blankness: a wall of nothing. He had no words for it. Beyond it, the world ceased. He backed away.

The sky flared up behind him, and there was a rustling crash as the farmhouse roof fell in. Sparks leapt from the straw. Blood red from the inferno within and without, the dragon reared up and screamed in triumph.

40

Flight

Wearily, Tarcorax lifted his staff for the last time. A weak thread of light fluttered away from it and was lost.

'Run! Run!' cried Gamaran.

Dashing up to the Sorcerer and his daughter, he tried to pull them away. They seemed unable to move. His strength increased by terror, Gamaran dragged them roughly aside – only just in time. As the dragon's searing breath flared out, the earth sizzled where they had been standing.

A small black figure shot past Gamaran. It was Tulip, armed with a knitting needle. Darting over to the dragon's leg, she stabbed it hard. The giant leg twitched irritably, as if stung by an insect, and sent her tumbling away across the grass.

Silas hobbled over to help her up. The dragon's head veered down to watch them. The huge red eye blinked balefully. The dragon drew breath; but before it could disgorge its fire, someone else distracted it.

'Don't leave me behind, Silas!' cried Saintly Gran. 'Don't go without me! I'm coming with you this time! Wait!' She stumbled into the dragon's path. Right in front of it, she halted, bewildered by its stink and shadow, but unafraid; and stared, unseeing, straight into its eyes.

For a disconcerted second, the dragon flicked its head back. In that instant, Gamaran seized Gran and hauled her, noisily protesting, out of danger.

Rab gripped his ornate sword more tightly. Here he was, the only person with a weapon, and the only one not fighting! He couldn't be outdone by two old ladies. What was the point in having a sword if he wasn't going to use it?

So although his energy and courage had long since evaporated, Rab made himself advance, sword outstretched, until the heat of the dragon's body battered at him. It was like standing too close to a bonfire: his front was scorched, his back was icy.

'All dragons have a soft spot in their bellies,' he told himself. 'That's what the stories say.' With all his might, he lunged with his sword straight at the scaly chest. The sword bent and buckled. Rab hung on to it – there was nothing else he could do – and jabbed at the surprised dragon again and again with the crumpled blade.

Roaring, the dragon tried to swipe him with its claws. The third swipe caught him round the waist and tipped him onto his back. Wasting no more time on Rab, the dragon lumbered towards the weary Sorcerer.

Rab curled up instinctively to avoid being trampled on, and felt a huge, clawed foot scrape past.

Suddenly the dragon stopped and screeched in anger. It was being attacked from the air.

Hieronymus had never flown before. His wings of glass had been designed for looks, not flight. But he flexed them now and they bore him painfully upwards. He could feel fine cracks spreading through his body at every wing beat, yet he flew on. As the dragon bore down on his master, he flew in its face, slashing at its eyes with his razor-sharp glass talons. The dragon, rearing, tossed its head and screeched once more – this time, in a long, harsh shriek of pain.

Rab, beneath the dragon's belly, tried to stab upwards. His useless sword served no purpose but to remind the dragon he was there. The dragon's foot stamped on him and pinned him to the ground. He struggled fruitlessly, gasping at its heat.

Abruptly the dragon lurched sideways. Porphyry had joined the assault. The pig's teeth – much stronger than Rab's sword – had fastened on its ankle.

The dragon bellowed in exasperation. Spitting a wild funnel of fire that missed the humans entirely, it shook its body convulsively to try and rid itself of its tormentors. Its great wing buffeted Hieronymus from the air. The glass gryphon was dashed to the ground, and shattered into a thousand tinkling pieces. The dragon caught up the screaming pig, raked its belly open with a claw, and sent it flying through the air into the darkness. The screaming stopped.

41

The Dawn Walker

She had not expected that the Dawn Walker should look so ordinary. Even cloaked and hooded, he was just a man striding through the moon-white mist.

I've got the wrong one, thought Freya as she followed him. This is just some tired farmer taking a short cut. *This* can't be the one whose eyes you may not meet. It can't be for *him* that all the gifts are left by the bedside, all the prayers whispered over the sick...

She followed him anyway, since she had come this far, keeping his slow-pacing figure just visible in front of her. The mist deadened all sounds: no noise from the battle reached her here. She was encased in unchanging fog, with nothing visible but the patch of ground beneath her feet and the Walker just ahead. She might as well have been on a grassy treadmill that rolled away unendingly, leaving her always in the same place.

The Walker faded momentarily, and she hurried forward until his figure was clear again. He was carrying something, she could see now: something large, wrapped in a grey cloth, that weighed him down and slowed his footsteps.

'Walker,' she said, and heard the mist swallow her words. 'Walker, wait for me!'

The Walker halted, but did not turn to face her. Freya hurried up to him and round to face him, sure now that she'd got the wrong one, just a farmer or a pedlar with his bundle. Of course the Dawn Walker wouldn't be here. He didn't exist.

She looked up into his eyes, as grey as a cold sea.

'You called me,' said the Dawn Walker, and the words crashed like waves through her head and seeped into her bones.

'I need your help,' said Freya numbly.

'I do not help the living.'

'But they've called a dragon,' said Freya. Cold was spreading through her, soaking her to her fingertips, making it hard to speak. 'It's destroying everything. It doesn't belong here. Can't you send it back?'

'I?'

'The Sorcerer can't do it. You're the only one powerful enough.'

'I do not help the living.'

'I'll give you,' said Freya, shivering helplessly, 'I'll give you my life, if you'll just take away the dragon. Please.'

The sea-grey eyes gazed at her consideringly, but then the reply came:

'It does not work that way.'

'You took my father's life. Take mine too.'

148

'Your father is not here,' said the Walker. For the first time, she thought she heard a hint of pity in his voice. 'You will not find him here. Go back. Keep your promise to those who need you.'

'But then how can I save them?'

'Not by dying.'

'Then how?'

'By caring.'

'But I don't understand! What can I do?'

'Have courage,' he said. 'It will not count for nothing.'

'But can't you help us?' Freya cried in despair.

'I may not be commanded.'

'But please—'

'I cannot be begged.' As he spoke, the Dawn Walker's eyes closed for a moment. Freya had a brief vision of an endless sea, of dark waves rolling in unceasingly to a shadowed shore. He looked so tired, thought Freya, more tired than she had ever been. Imagine walking forever through this fog, never setting eyes on the sun. And he was weighed down by his burden. Her pity outweighed her fear.

'Let me carry that, at least,' she said. 'It looks so heavy.' She reached out for it, and the cold rose through her as though she was sinking through deep water, but the Walker did not resist. He let the bundle, wrapped in its cloth, slide into her arms.

Freya staggered, for it was heavier than she expected: warm, dense and motionless. It smelled over-poweringly of pig.

The Walker was gliding away, but now she could not follow. With this weight in her arms, she could hardly move.

'Wait, stop!' she cried. 'I need to ask you—'

But he had disappeared into the mist, which closed behind him like a curtain. And now the mist began to shift and swirl. It gathered speed, although there was no wind, sweeping past Freya until she seemed to be rushing backwards through a cloud.

42

End

'Porphyry!' wailed the pig-girl. But the pig had gone. The white mist flooded out from the valley across the fields, with the cold dawn behind it: and it was into the mist that the pig had fallen.

The dragon towered over the petrified humans. It spread its wings in a huge, glowing arc, and lashed its tail. Rab, no longer trapped beneath its claws, began to inch away on hands and knees, but even as he crawled he knew that there was no escape. The dragon screeched above him in merciless fury.

Then the note of its cry altered. The end of its tail had whipped through the creeping white fog. The dragon lunged round, and a wing brushed through the mist. The dragon screamed in agony, a hundred times louder than the pig's final scream, and all the watchers (except for Gran) shuddered and stopped their ears.

Then they stiffened in amazement, as all (apart from Gran) perceived the dragon's wing begin to wither, like a dying leaf. They saw its incandescence fade, and flare, and fade again. Frantically the dragon twisted and turned, trying to free itself from the mist, but at every turn the drifting cloud swirled across another part of it.

In its legs, its tail, its head, the fire was slowly, inexorably dimmed. With crumpled wings, it sank onto its belly. Its tail fell limp. The glow in its eyes darkened, and went out.

Cold, grey and still, it lay surrounded by the dying glow of numerous small fires. The watchers stood silent for a while, uncertain. Then Rab darted forward and slashed at a great foot with his ruined sword – partly for revenge, and partly just to make sure. He almost expected the dragon to lurch back up with a snarl.

But at the sword's touch, the tough skin wrinkled and collapsed. It turned to paper, then dissolved to a fine ash that blew away. The change spread all along the dragon's body: its legs, its back, its tail greyed and crumbled and fell away as powder. A light wind rose to dissipate the dust.

Beneath the dissolving skin, a white framework began to appear. The dragon's bones were gradually revealed, until the giant skeleton stood bare and frozen before them.

Rab lifted his sword again, and promptly dropped it. Somehow, it had straightened out. All its ornate carvings and jewels had gone. It had become plain and dull, and very sharp; and it weighed a ton.

'It wasn't me that killed it, was it?' he said unsurely.

Tarcorax stared intently at the wall of mist. It was receding now as the wind tugged at its edges. From it, a figure was emerging.

'No,' he said. 'No, that wasn't you.'

152

43

Sunrise

The mist swirled away, retreating back into the river valley. In the east, a bright fingernail of sun was sitting on the edge of the world. Freya walked out of the cloud into a smoky dawn.

Her heavy bundle wriggled suddenly in its cloth and kicked her sharply on the arm. Then it squirmed down from her grasp, and, shaking itself, trotted over the burnt ground to the pig-girl.

Amaranth gasped. She fell on her knees and buried her face in Porphyry's neck. But Tarcorax walked slowly up to Freya and touched her very gently on the shoulder, as if afraid that she might dissolve and crumble like the dragon.

Freya barely noticed. She looked beyond him at the ruined farmhouse, the remnants of the laboriously thatched roof still smoking. She saw Gran in the doorway, leaning on the pirate's arm, while he patted her hand.

'I'll look after you this time,' he was saying. 'I've left

you for too long. This time we'll run away to sea together. How about it?' Gran smiled and nodded.

Beside them, Freya saw an old woman in a squashed black hat, beaming from ear to ear. She began to cackle excitedly.

'Well, that's the stuff to give 'em! That's the *real* thing! A spell straight out of the stories, that is! Dust and ashes! My word!'

Freya's gaze passed over her and stopped on Rab, who was dragging a long sword across the grass.

'Now that's a real dragon-slaying sword!' declared the witch with satisfaction. 'You're a proper hero now, whether you like it or not!'

'But I can't even lift it,' said Rab, sounding worried.

Freya looked on past him and saw Gamaran, whose face shone back at her full of joy and tears.

'Can I stay and learn about sheep?' he asked her. 'I'll write you a poem. I'll write you hundreds.'

Freya felt dizzy. She swayed a little, and stepped sideways onto something that crunched.

Tarcorax stooped to pick it up. It was a piece of glass; a shard of Hieronymus. Carefully the Sorcerer gathered up more fragments, cradling them in his hand.

'So many pieces!' he said sadly. 'Poor Hieronymus. I should have taken better care of him.'

'You should have taken better care of everything,' the witch said acidly.

Amaranth raised her head from hugging the pig. 'You can always make him again.'

'Not the way he was.'

154

'Yes, you can! I'll help you. We'll make him stronger than before. Reinforce the glass. Make him able to fly properly; and maybe even run without breaking.'

'Could we?' asked the Sorcerer doubtfully.

She stood up straighter. 'Why not? We could rebuild the Glass Palace too – but with improvements.'

'Less glass,' said Tarcorax hopefully.

'No dungeons,' added Amaranth.

'It'll take a long time,' said Tarcorax. 'Years, maybe.' He did not sound as if he minded much. 'But where can we live meanwhile?'

'You can try a house, like everyone else,' said the witch, 'and high time too.'

'Then you'll have to get rid of the pig,' Tarcorax told his daughter.

Her face took on a stony look. 'The pig that just gave its life for you? No pig, no deal.'

Tarcorax looked long at Porphyry, nosing under the shattered oak for roasted acorns. Then he stroked his beard, and glanced awkwardly at Gamaran, Silas, Tulip and Rab.

'All of you nearly gave your lives,' he muttered. 'I suppose, for that, I must allow you your lives back. You are all pardoned, fully and permanently. The Rules are repealed.'

'All of them?' asked Rab, astounded.

'Not all of them! I'll think about it. Don't rush me! A land needs some Rules. And people need to obey them.' He glared around at everyone in general.

'You only need one Rule,' said Tulip. 'Help each

other out. That covers the lot, don't you think?'

'Rules are made to be broken,' declared Amaranth.

'Absolute rubbish!' roared Tarcorax. 'And if you must keep that pig, it goes in a sty.'

'Then I do too.'

'Not while you're my daughter!'

'Here we go again,' said the witch. 'Playing their little games. Seesaw, spin around, argy-bargy, all fall down. Heaven help us.' She winked at Freya. 'Swapping a dragon's life for a pig's, eh? How did you persuade the Walker to make the trade?'

Freya gazed at her wordlessly.

'No one bargains with the Walker, not in any story I've ever heard.' Tulip shook her head in baffled admiration. 'So who's the hero in this one?'

Freya regarded the dragon's bones. They arched high over her: as bare as a shipwreck, as smooth as driftwood, as rosy as a shell in the first clear rays of the rising sun. She would have to look at them every time she opened the farmhouse door.

Rab dropped the sword. He said, 'I think I'd better come back home for a while, and mend the well.'

'Yes,' said Freya. 'Oh, yes. I think you better had.'